Moontide—where the past buried its secrets, along with its dead . . .

"There is something about this house—so big and dark and, well, desolate! It's as though something tragic or evil had happened here. Are old houses, do you think, affected by the things that go on under their roofs? Can you see and feel old sadnesses and crimes in places, as you can in people?"

She knew she was babbling, but she couldn't seem to stop. And while she had been pouring out all that idiocy, his face had been changing. When she stopped at last, his features were cool and stiff; he seemed to have withdrawn behind a mask and left only an expressionless façade before her.

There were other things she wanted to tell him, but she could not remember what they were. She watched him leave, her apprehensions stronger than ever now. She had to get back to Mrs. Aldrich; she had to go up the badly lighted staircase, and walk the length of the gloomy hall. Hand outstretched, as though to ward off the evil, she ran up to the landing.

Abruptly, she halted. A long, formless shadow had fallen across her path. . . .

Moon of Darkness

Miriam Lynch

PINNACLE BOOKS LOS ANGELES

This is a work of fiction. All the characters and events portrayed in this book are fictional, and any resemblance to real people or incidents is purely coincidental.

MOON OF DARKNESS

A Pinnacle Books edition, published by special arrangement with the author's agent.

Jay Garon-Brooke Associates
415 Central Park West, 17D
New York, N.Y. 10025

ISBN: 0-523-40-167-1

First printing, December 1977

Cover illustration by Adrian Osterling

Printed in the United States of America

PINNACLE BOOKS, INC.
One Century Plaza
2029 Century Park East
Los Angeles, California 90067

MOON OF DARKNESS

1

Nightfall came suddenly. One minute, it seemed, the world was bathed in the lemon-colored glow of dusk and then, in the next, was swallowed up in darkness.

It was a good thing, Rosalie told herself, that she was not nervous about driving alone on a strange road. A little tight-nerved, yes. Always, taking a new case, there was that feeling. And the director of the nurses' registry had been—well, a little odd about this one. "It should be only for a few days. You can stick it out for that long, I know you can, Miss Dexter. I'll tell you the truth. We had a couple of other girls on it and they quit. But the patient is terminal and, as I said, it won't be for long."

She had given Rosalie directions for reaching the place where an old woman lay dying. "You can't miss the house—Moontide. It's rather remote but there's a road at the further end of the village that leads directly to it."

Rosalie had had no trouble finding the road that turned and ran through a point of land that stretched out over and was surrounded by the ocean. She could hear the faint thunder of the surf and, even with the car window rolled up, smell the salt air, and she knew that she could not be very far from Moontide, the only house she had ever heard of that had a name.

She was conscious of a little ache of tiredness and she wished now that she had not accepted this case, coming as soon as it did after her last one. It was not the money nor a desire to accommodate the registry director; it had presented itself as a form of therapy.

When you were thrown by a horse, you were supposed to get up immediately and mount again. When you had a car accident, you hurried to get behind the wheel once more. Her last patient had died. There was still a small, hovering sadness when she thought about Hugo Bannister's death. She was not supposed to feel that way of course. What was the old nursing school phrase? "Sympathy but not empathy." She had not remembered it nor lived by it during the weeks she had taken care of Mr. Bannister, that erudite, good-humored, gentle-mannered man. That he had succumbed while she was having a day off, coupled regret with personal sorrow.

Rosalie had never been able to take casually the death of a patient, and here she was on her way to care for another terminal case, one which would be of only a few days' duration. But this one was different. Zena Aldrich was in her nineties. Her organs were failing. All Rosalie could do for her was to keep her comfortable for the short time remaining to her.

And it will be different this time, Rosalie told herself. I will not have enough time to really become acquainted with her or personally interested in her, even if I let myself fall into that trap again. Even if I haven't learned my lesson.

She let the picture of Hugo Bannister slip into her mind once more. His keen eyes twinkled at her. His fine, aristocratic features and the slivers of silvery hair across a pale scalp seemed so real she almost believed that she was seeing him again. Then she banished the image, vowed she would not let herself get neurotic about him. It had not been her fault that she had not been there when he died. The last heart attack before the fatal one had been so severe he had needed a private duty nurse. It was certain that she would not have been able to stave off death if she had been with him.

Requiem for Hugo Bannister. She let him slip into the mists of memory as something more immediate claimed her thoughts. The car gave a sudden lurch, listed and went bumping along for a few feet, and she knew that she had a flat tire.

She pulled into the side of the road and took her flashlight out of the glove compartment. Of course she was right, the tire was hopelessly flat, and she was not going to try to change it; not in her clean white uniform and certainly not in the darkness with no one to hold the flashlight while she struggled with a jack, spare and tire wrench. She had, after all, only two hands.

The house could not be far. It seemed that she had come quite a distance along this miserable lane with its coating of ground clam shells—she could see them now in the ray of her flashlight—that were death on old rubber. She could walk the rest of the way.

She got her suitcase from the back seat and the

two starched uniform caps, one on top of the other, from the front seat. Then she began to trudge up the lane.

At first she could not see anything much, only the narrow path of light that she spread in front of her. Then finally, as though rising from the cliffs at the end of the point of land, the house began to loom.

This was Moontide, the house that had been built a century ago by Ezra Thayer—so Rosalie had heard, had known about since her childhood. Try as she would, she could not remember ever hearing much more about the man, only that he had been one of the whaling captains who sailed their ships to the Orient and brought back its treasures to fill their big, newly constructed homes in the seacoast town of Stoneport.

They still stood, those stately graceful homes on the oceanfront. They stood proudly with their tall windows, fanlit doors and rooftop "widows' walks." The descendants of the sea captains lived in them. The little village was a world removed from Rosalie Dexter's small industrial town, and although she lived within five miles of them, she had never been in one of the big, white, beautiful houses until she had gone, in her capacity as a nurse, to Hugo Bannister's.

There he was in her mind again, and she set her face forward and resolved to forget her uneasiness over his death. She could see Moontide more clearly now. It was not like the other big houses in the village. On this wind-chilled October night with racing and broken clouds forming a background for its silhouette, it looked uncompromisingly ugly.

Instead of a widow's walk, there was an octagon-shaped cupola on its roof. Bay windows bristled from its lower story but the upper ones were stark and unadorned. When she came directly to it and with her vision adjusted to the gloom, she could see that its shingles, once doubtlessly painted white, had become shriveled and silvered by the storms and sun-baking of the years.

She stood hesitating for a moment. The sound of the surf was louder now as it came roaring up the rocks and fell back, hissing. The salt-laden wind swept around her and lifted the corners of her coat and a pervasive chill spread through every part of her body. And the dark night seemed to hold something ominous that frightened her.

She wished now that she had waited until morning to come to Moontide. Her rushing off the minute she got the call from the registry seemed like lunacy. She had an impulse to return home and come back when it was daylight, but that would be even more insane. She was here now. For better or for worse. And why, she asked herself, had that foolish phrase popped into her mind?

The lane had become a driveway that curved to the front of the house and then away from it. Steps led down to it and beyond them was a huge door with intricately carved grillwork forming the top half of it.

A bell or chimes or knocker of some sort had to be somewhere among the decorative ironwork but while Rosalie was searching for it, the door swung open and light from the hall beyond it poured out. She could not see, at first, the face of the small, shrunken woman who stood there peering out at her. It was not until they both stepped into the hall that she had a good look at the little creature who had admitted her.

She had a dark brown face wrinkled like slashed worn leather. In spite of her age, her hair was black and shiny. Her features were somewhat coarse and thick, and she wore a pair of thick-lensed eyeglasses which did not seem to belong on her face. She had her head thrust forward, so that she looked like an inquisitive bird, as she peered at Rosalie.

Ill-at-ease and with the silence making her even more uncomfortable, the girl said, "I am Rosalie Dexter. I'm to be Mrs. Aldrich's nurse."

The old woman said only one word. "Azie," and she pointed at her own chest. Then she shuffled backward, motioning. Midway down the hall, she halted. Out of the shadows there, shuffling along from the back of the house, came the hulking figure of a man. He towered over both the other two, and he was dark-skinned, like the woman, and he was powerfully built. He lifted Rosalie's suitcase with a single sweep of his arms and placed it on his shoulder. With his height and strength and the mahogany tone of his skin—a shade lighter than the old woman's—he was an arresting figure. But there was a slackness of his mouth and a blankness in his eyes that Rosalie recognized immediately with a surging of pity.

The woman pointed to him. "Jug. Mine."

By which Rosalie guessed that he was her son

and her pity now was for a mother's heartache. People like Jug were seldom aware of their own lacks. She hoped that he would understand when she told him about the car she had left in the lane and the need for its tire to be changed. "The keys," she said, "are still in the ignition," and he merely stared back at her vacantly.

Azie muttered, "Upstairs," and turned and led the way down the long, badly lighted hall in the direction of the staircase that curved up from it. Rosalie had no opportunity for anything more than a passing glimpse at the huge sea chest that stood against one wall, a Chinese vase on a teak table, the muted colors of hanging tapestries.

The carpet under her feet felt soft and velvety and the handrail of the banister was of some rich, polished wood. But the flight of stairs that led to the third floor was bare and steep and narrow. Nor was there any covering on the long corridor; it threw back echoes of footsteps and only a single, low watt bulb did anything at all to dispel its darkness.

There seemed to be leading from this hall other passages so she guessed that the house had ells or additions but she could not see into them and she did not have time to pause and examine her surroundings because Azie was hurrying ahead with surprising spryness.

She stopped at a door far down the hall and took a bunch of keys from her apron pocket. "Your room," she said. She turned on a light switch and the room bloomed into brightness which was dazzling after the gloom outside.

It was a comfortable, old-fashioned room with

a high bed, faded chintz draperies, two small, cretonne-covered chairs and a massive dresser with a good mirror over it. It had a subtle, musty smell that closed-up rooms near the ocean often do.

Jug put the suitcase on the bed and the two left silently. For Rosalie, the task of unpacking lay ahead but she was in no hurry to begin it. She went to the mirror and looked at her image. When she saw the anxious, intent expression in the eyes that looked back at her, she grinned sheepishly.

So all right, she told herself, admit the truth and shame the devil. The fact of the matter is that you came here not because of all that therapy jazz; that was just a byproduct, not the real reason, was it? And it wasn't because of the money and you were sort of thinking about a couple of weeks vacation. Why you really came was Doctor Sargent.

The director of the registry had said, "It's Doctor Sargent's case," and within ten minutes Rosalie had been ironing fresh uniforms, buffing her white shoes, evading her mother's probing questions.

"But why now, dear? Surely the morning would be time enough! Why do you have to go rushing off at this time of night?"

If she had been honest, she would have told her mother, "Because I'm half in love with Richard Sargent, just like every other rattle-brained nurse at Baker Memorial Hospital. I haven't even seen him to speak to since I was on a case there six months ago. I've passed him a few times, his car going in one direction and mine in another and we've waved. That's all."

Or, if she had been completely honest, she might have said, "Maybe when he sees me alone, away from all those other nurses—really sees me, I mean—he'll discover that I'm someone he wants to know better."

What she was trying to do now, as she leaned forward and looked at herself in the mirror, was see herself as Dr. Richard Sargent would see her when he made his next call on his patient. She tried to score herself objectively.

Eyes, good: they were a quiet shade of green and the lashes were long enough and thick enough that she was never tempted to try the kind that came in little plastic boxes at cosmetic counters.

Skin, excellent: it was firm and creamy and sometimes the color rose under it, and that annoyed her because she thought she must be the last blushing female left in the world.

Hair—it was a matter of opinion: either you liked auburn hair or you didn't. At least she was grateful that it had darkened from the carrotty color of her childhood. She wore it simply and cut short for the sake of her cap.

Nose, hopeless; she never got any further in her optimism than her nose because it turned up in a way that she considered ridiculous in a grown woman, and it seemed to pull her short upper lip with it. A man had once described her nose as "piquant." She loathed the word.

So this was what Dr. Richard Sargent saw when he looked at her—if he ever actually did. She remembered his alert, no-nonsense manner, his polite but impersonal way of speaking, and the faint air of aloofness that was probably his protective barrier that kept away from a handsome, eligible young doctor all romance-minded nurses and female patients.

If she actually had come with the idea of promoting a closer relationship with Doctor Sargent, then the whole thing was an exercise in insanity. The eyes in the mirror grew grave and uneasy. There was something Rosalie hadn't liked about the house from the very first.

She was not given to foolish fancies but she thought she could feel something—an undercurrent of unhappiness or a depressing aura that seemed to prevade the place. Perhaps it was the imminent death of the woman who had lived in it all her ninety-odd years. An approaching demise might cause just such a dark and disturbing atmosphere.

At any rate, Rosalie reflected, she had better things to do than stand in front of the mirror moping over her reflection and dreaming up ideas about vibrations in the house. She had a patient to care for.

No one had told her where the sickroom was, but when she had finished unpacking and bathed her hands and face and freshened her makeup, she found it easily enough. It was on the floor below her own bedroom; its door was open and she could see the dim light filtering out of it as she went along the second floor hall.

It, too, was at the end of a corridor where a closed door evidently led to another passage. It was a tall, square room with many windows that had heavy draperies pulled across them. There was an enormous bed with a carved headboard. There were several small chairs with fraying upholstery and a thick and ugly flowered rug. There was the unmistakable sickroom smell.

Zena Aldrich seemed almost lost among the huge pillows and thick quilts of her bed. Her face looked very dark against the whiteness of the bed-linen. Old people's skin sometimes darkened as they approached the ends of their lives, Rosalie knew, and it was saddening to look down upon the wrinkled, nut-brown face in its last hours.

She touched the withered hand that lay outside the bedclothes. It felt as dry and crisp as old paper. The sparse, still-black eyelashes fluttered briefly, but Zena Aldrich's eyes did not open.

Rosalie could see, even by a superficial examination, that death was very close. The woman's breathing was shallow, her lips had a bluish tint. She was almost in a comatose condition.

Someone had been taking very good care of her. The white, wispy hair was immaculate and the wasted skin smelled of soap and lotion.

Who? Rosalie wondered. Who had bathed her and changed her nightgown and kept her propped on her pillows? Someone, evidently, who loved her had performed these little acts to keep her comfortable. But who had it been?

The question seemed to be answered a moment later when a young, strikingly pretty girl rushed into the room and cried out in relief, "Oh, thank God you're here! I heard someone. I hoped it would be a nurse."

She was, she said, Gloria Aldrich, the patient's great-granddaughter.

"All she has, really. There are just the two of us

left of the family. I live here, of course. We've tried to do what we could for her but she needs a professional nurse and we haven't had one since—since the other one left. What is your name?"

When Rosalie told her and added, "I'll be on twenty-four hour duty as long as she needs me," the lovely, fair-skinned face lost none of its look of strain and distress.

Gloria Aldrich cried out, in a voice that had hoarsened, "Please, please, Miss Dexter, you've got to save her! You mustn't let her die!"

Her hands were twisting and her eyes pleaded, and Rosalie was at a loss as to how to answer the dramatic outburst. The girl must know, of course, that there was no hope for her great-grandmother. She said gently, "She is very old. And her organs are in failure. It can only be a matter of time."

"No! No!" The face became even more anguished, the voice more distraught. "She can't die! You mustn't let her! You have to keep her alive!"

Tears rose in a flood, spilled out from the swimming eyes. Rosalie stared at her silently. She was upset by the girl's overpowering grief, but there was something else, too, that disturbed her.

She had a nagging feeling of puzzlement that had begun the moment she had had her first full look into Gloria Aldrich's face. It seemed, somehow, familiar although she was certain that she had never seen this girl before. A picture in the newspaper? But it wasn't that, and they had never met in person. The path of a hard-working nurse, daughter of middle-class parents, would never have crossed that of Moontide's rich and aristocratic heiress.

Then, suddenly, she realized why she had seemed to recognize Gloria Aldrich. Only a short time before she had been staring at her own image in the mirror. "Why," she thought, astonished, "we look a great deal alike."

It was true. Gloria's hair was a shade lighter than her own, more Titian red than auburn. But they both had the same sort of fine skin, similar delicate features even to the tip-tilted noses, almost identically-shaped bodies, and they were practically the same height.

Gloria, drying her eyes, became aware, too, of the resemblance. She said with a forced smile, "You know something? You and I look enough alike to be sisters!" and Rosalie nodded and turned back to her patient. The likeness between them seemed frivolous and unimportant in the face of the fact that this emotional young girl expected her to perform a miracle and rescue from death the old woman who was so plainly marked for it.

"I will do my best," she said, her voice flat, "but nursing can do just so much. She cannot recover, of course. You must know that it's only a matter of time."

She heard the last word echoed in a gasp. "Time!"

Gloria backed away and fled, leaving Rosalie alone with her puzzlement. Then she pushed that and everything else except concern for her patient out of her mind. She knew how little she could do for this woman, but what little it was must be performed conscientiously.

She searched for the doctor's orders on the bedside table, on the tall dresser, on the lowboy; and she could not find them. Nor was there any medication in sight. While she was waiting for Doctor Sargent to come or for Gloria Aldrich to return, all she could do to make Mrs. Aldrich comfortable was to change the bedclothes, bathe her, put her into a clean nightgown, if she could find one.

Nobody, Rosalie thought a little pettishly, had given her instructions how to find anything. Azie, the servant, and her childlike son, had left her hastily once she was shown to her room. Gloria Aldrich, the girl who wept so copiously over her great-grandmother's coming death, had not bothered to relay the doctor's orders nor to point out the linen closet.

No matter. She would find it herself. She had seen the open door of a bathroom a little further down the hall. The linen closet could not be far away.

The second floor corridor was so badly lighted that Rosalie did not see the worn spot on its carpet and caught her heel. She almost fell, was saved only by throwing out her hand and balancing herself against the wall. That would be all I'd need, she thought wryly, to break a leg. There was actual physical danger here in the near darkness. She did not have to dream up things like menacing atmospheres or ominous auras.

She found the closet by opening door after door, most of them leading into empty or badly furnished rooms until she came upon the right one.

The linen closet was deep and narrow. She could see the sparsely stacked shelves at the further end of it and she walked in and reached her hands up toward them. Then she heard a sound, like a small explosion, behind her. As she whirled, she heard something else—the snapping of a lock into place.

She cried, "Now wait a minute!" but she knew, even before she put her hand on the doorknob that the effort was useless. The door, big and heavy and solid, as all the doors in this house seemed to be, would not move, even though she turned the knob and pushed with all her weight.

And although she cried out, until her throat grew raw and aching. and although she beat her hands on the door until they felt bruised and sore, no one came in answer to her shouting.

She knew that she had been deliberately locked into the linen closet. And she knew something else, too—that it would not be long before the oxygen in this small space was used up and that she would succumb to suffocation. And that she would die here as someone had intended that she would.

2

THERE CAME THE PANIC, the near hysteria and, slowly, the numbing despair. And then, finally, the creeping lethargy and with it the drowsiness that would grow heavier and heavier until, she knew, the end came.

Rosalie felt it enveloping her and gathering her up into blackness, and she knew that she must struggle to make one last effort or she would be completely lost. She forced her body upward and she fell against the door. She pounded upon it with every last ounce of strength she had left and she forced out her voice to shout, "Help! Help! I'm locked in here!"

Over the tattooing of her fists and the crying of her voice, she could hear nothing. She was about to sink back onto the floor, all hope gone, when the door opened suddenly. She went plunging through it and sprawled out onto the floor beyond.

She lay there, gulping and sobbing, caring only that she was free of that horrible confinement and not at first, that someone had come to rescue her. That someone had strong hands. They fastened themselves around her and lifted her to her feet. She clutched at their owner and when her vision cleared, she saw that she was staring into the man's face. It belonged to Dr. Richard Sargent.

In the gloomy light of the hall, she became

aware of his frown. She heard him say, "What the heck is all this?"

It took her a little while to speak. Her throat was still clogged and her tongue felt as though it were swollen to twice its normal size. She went on clutching at the doctor's coat and finally she managed to get out a few words.

"Somebody locked me into the closet. Somebody tried to kill me!"

As she stood there blinking in an effort to regain her composure, she saw the expression of his face change from puzzlement to blankness. Something seemed to fall down over his features, a cold stiffness. As though she had slipped out of her own body and, detached, could observe them, her mind registered a picture of the two of them. A girl in a rumpled uniform, its skirt smeared from the dust on the floor, her hair plastered damply against her forehead, her eyes wild. He in his impeccable clothing gazing at the disheveled creature with a chilled and chilling disbelief.

His mouth opened and when he had spoken, closed again smartly with the precision of a steel trap. "You're Miss Dexter? You must be. The registry informed me that you would be here."

She could almost read his thoughts. Because he was an extremely attractive man—tall, wide-shouldered, strongly-cut features, a sensitive mouth, crisp and closely cut hair—all the women he met must have tried all sorts of tricks to attract his attention. He would be wary; she could not blame him for that. No doubt he believed that she had ascertained the hour of his house calls. Probably he had jumped to the conclusion that she had dreamed up an idiotic ruse so that their first meeting here in this house would have a dramatic and unforgettable impact.

Her brain buzzed, half in indignation, half in desperation to make him see the error in his thinking.

As though she would go to such lengths . . .

She suddenly became dizzy. Everything swung around in blackness. When her wits returned, she found that he was holding her stiffly and she saw that his face had not changed at all. He still wore that remote and cautious expression.

She would have liked to remain there against him, even though his embrace was an unwilling one, but her pride returned and she stepped away from him and said in a thin, squeaking voice, "It is true, you know. I went into the closet for some linen and somebody—somebody who must have been following me—came up behind me and locked me in. I heard the latch snap. And then for a long time—oh, it did really seem like a long time!—I was in there and I couldn't get out. I would have suffocated if you hadn't come." She looked steadily into his eyes. "You do believe me, don't you?"

"That you were locked in—sure. But it was undoubtedly an accident. These old houses . . . springs on the doors . . . the wind."

She shook her head. There was no place for a breeze to come through in that long, dark hall. She had shut the other doors after opening them in her search for the linen closet. She tried to tell him that but he had turned away and was striding along the corridor, his black bag swinging at his side, on his way to Zena Aldrich's bedroom.

He was crisp and businesslike as he gave her his orders. The medication was for the purpose of keeping the patient quiet as much as possible. She was to be turned frequently and kept propped on pillows to facilitate breathing. "Although it will not matter very much now, I suppose. It may be only hours, or a few days at the very most."

There came back into Rosalie's mind the memory of Gloria Aldrich's anguished cry. "You must keep her alive!"

She asked, "There's no chance at all of pulling her through?" and Doctor Sargent looked at her as though she were a babbling lunatic. He said shortly, "When she's this far in failure? Of course not. You must know that, Miss Dexter."

So I have lost more points, she thought. It must be some sort of record for the short length of time.

He spoke again. "She was dying when I came onto the case a few weeks ago. And after all, I'm only a physician, not God."

So all right, she answered him silently, I'm an idiot. A lame-brain who locks herself into closets and a nurse who can't see what's in front of her eyes.

She was furious with them both, herself most of all for allowing his attitude to matter so much to her. But after he left, she went on thinking about him and decided that if she had deliberately tried, she couldn't have done more to get off on the wrong foot.

The night was long and quiet and monotonous. She sat in a chair by the bedside, dozing from time to time. During one of the periods of restless sleeping, she dreamed of Richard. She came awake feeling shamed, but she could not help wondering how soon it would be before he came again.

He came in the morning. He told Rosalie, with economy of words, that he was in the habit of making two calls a day. Mrs. Aldrich's great-granddaughter had requested it, he said, and Rosalie thought she detected a softened note in his voice when he spoke of Gloria.

He did not utter a single personal word to her, Rosalie. There were no inquiries about her recovery from her ordeal in the linen closet. He did not mention her belief that an attempt had been made on her life. Patently, he had never put any credence in it.

Rosalie, after the sort of night of duty which was so familiar to her, was not now quite so convinced of it, either. In the morning, as she changed her uniform in the room upstairs, with the gilded sunlight streaming in through the windows, she began to think that possibly what Doctor Sargent had said was true. Attempted murder, on this quiet day when the sea outside was only a faraway murmur, was something beyond the scope of her imaginings.

Perhaps it had been an accident, nothing more than a heavy, old door swinging shut under its own weight. As for the lack of response to her pounding and screaming, doubtlessly no one had been able to hear her from one of the other floors.

She had taken it for granted, without giving the matter any real thought, that the only occupants of the house besides her and her patient were

Azie and Jug and Gloria Aldrich. At luncheon she learned differently.

Azie had served her a tray at breakfast time. At noon she came to announce, "You eat in dining room. With others. I stay here with her," and she pointed at the woman in the bed.

Rosalie went downstairs and the others in the dining room were Gloria and two young people she had not seen before. There was a girl about the same age as Gloria and herself who said with a winning little smile, "I'm Julie Merrick, sort of a relative. And this is Tony Chandler."

Gloria put in hastily, moving possessively to his side, "My fiance."

He was a slender young man with easily moving, beautiful hands and a very white smile and the darkest hair Rosalie had ever seen. He and Gloria made a striking contrast with their different coloring; together, they made the handsomest of couples.

Julie Merrick was dark, too, almost as tall as Tony, and she had a round, childishly sweet face and a great mane of shining black hair. Her eyes were clear hazel, large and long, and in them and in her smile there was a please-like-me anxiety.

Rosalie, in her uniform, felt a little like a country cousin in the presence of these three beautiful young people, each with a special, individual form of good looks. But it was to her that Tony began to address all his remarks when they were at the table.

At first she believed that the attention he was pouring upon her was part of his flawless manners, that he was sorry for her and attempting to make her feel at ease and included in the group.

"Do you have everything you need for your stay here? Can we do anything to make you more comfortable?"

And then came the more personal question. "Where did you train?" and "Did you always want to be a nurse?" and "Isn't it rather a hard profession for a sensitive girl?"

And then it got even more personal. "Isn't it too bad that Mrs. Aldrich can't appreciate the fact that she had someone as lovely as you decorating her sickroom?" and "Did anyone ever tell you that your eyes are the exact shade of emeralds in certain lights?"

Rosalie squirmed and slid her glance away from him and, trying to escape his eyes, found that she could not help meeting those of Gloria who sat directly across the table from her. Gloria, Rosalie saw, looked like a punished child. Her face was suffering; her mouth seemed to be becoming wounded from the biting of her teeth into her lips.

Each time Tony paid one of his extravagant compliments to Rosalie, Gloria winced. And Julie Merrick, sitting at the other end of the table, was missing none of it. She did not say anything at all, but her long-lashed eyes raised whenever Tony spoke and she kept smiling at him, and at the others, with her sweet and gentle smile.

It was plain that Gloria was very much in love with Tony. Everything in her manner seemed to shout it. She scarcely took her eyes from his face. She leaned toward him in a way that begged him to notice her. She smiled eagerly when he threw a careless word or glance in her direction.

Rosalie grew more and more uncomfortable. Perhaps if I ignore him he will lose interest, she thought, and even her monosyllabic replies stopped abruptly. She was aching with pity for Gloria. She pretended that she did not hear Tony when he said, "We must see to it that your stay here isn't all work. You have to have some time off now and then, right?"

Under other circumstances, she might have been flattered. A girl like her did not have a man like Tony Chandler making a play for her every day in the week.

A man like Tony Chandler. The moment she had heard his name, she knew who he was. That name got into the newspapers at least once a week. He was on all sorts of civic committees in Stoneport and in the state, he was a member of a very old and very prominent family. He was an amateur champion golfer, a pilot of his own plane, a surf rider, sky diver, scuba diver, director of a bank and several other businesses and organizations, commodore of the Yacht Club.

It was odd, Rosalie mused, that in view of all the other things she had read about him, she had not seen anything in the newspapers about his engagement to Gloria Aldrich. It was the sort of thing—two handsome young people of the inner social circle, the town's most eligible bachelor and the heiress to Moontide—that should have been splashed all over the front pages of not only the local newspaper but those of the big city ones as well.

Perhaps it had been. Perhaps she had missed it. But, no, if it had been a recent news story, Hugo Bannister would have pointed it out to her. He must have been of the same social set as the Chandlers and the Aldriches.

Oddly enough, at that moment Gloria spoke of Hugo Bannister. "A friend of my father's. You took care of him, didn't you, Miss Dexter? I was down there to see him one day—I guess it must have been during your time off. But he spoke of you. Very glowingly, I might add."

Rosalie said, on a little wave of sadness, "He was my last case. I was very fond of him. A kind, gentle man and a wonderful patient. And so interested in life, in everything. Did you know he was writing a book? You can't imagine his enthusiasm about it during the last days he was working on it."

They were all silent for a few minutes. Even Tony seemed subdued. In her anxiety to forestall any more personal conversation, Rosalie turned to Julie Merrick, who had seemed to be left out of things, somehow, all during the meal.

"You live here, too, Miss Merrick? All the time?"

Julie laughed a quiet little laugh. "God forbid! Not in the winter, I'm not that rugged. This place is really wild then, the tides and all. Sometimes they come up over the road and the house is cut off. But it's something else again in the summer. Really great. The yacht club, you know. I love sailing," and her eyes met Tony's briefly.

Then she went on, "I'm really sort of a waif. No real home except this one, and given a bed out of the kindness of Gloria's heart." Her smile became self-mocking. "I'm not real family so she could throw me out any time. Gloria's father married my mother when they were both over fifty. They're both dead now but I still hang around."

A little silence fell over the table while the two stepsisters exchanged glances that had nothing of affection in them. In fact, Rosalie noted with a little shock of surprise, there was in them something of not only antipathy but thinly veiled hostility. She felt the undercurrent of anger and it made her shiver.

Tony said lightly, "That's nutty. You are family. And the old place wouldn't be the same without you. You just better stick around. Right, Glo honey?"

Gloria had no choice but to nod and when she spoke, her voice sounded choked. "Yes," she said. "Of course, Tony."

But he was paying no attention to her. He was smiling at the other girl and something invisible seemed to wrap them together and close out the rest of the world. To Rosalie it was the most uncomfortable moment she had ever endured. Her heart ached for Gloria who looked as though she had been struck.

Julie wore a faint air of triumph all during the rest of that long, drawn-out meal during which Gloria kept jumping up to serve since Azie was keeping vigil in the sickroom. No hour had ever seemed longer and less enjoyable. And Rosalie recognized the reason.

She was in the room with two girls and the man they were both in love with; you did not need a ton of bricks to fall on you to realize that.

Gloria, in a valiant effort to keep the conversation going, asked Rosalie, "How was Grandma this morning? Does there seem to be any improvement?"

At that point, Julie leaned forward and listened intently for the answer. For some reason, it seemed extremely important to her although Rosalie could not guess why. Unless she, too, were extraordinarily fond of the old woman. Her head swung back and forth, like a spectator's at a tennis match, while Rosalie kept explaining, as gently as she could, that Zena Aldrich could not possibly last much longer, and Gloria kept refusing to believe it.

"You must do something, Miss Dexter! You must save her! She mustn't be allowed to die!"

Julie went on listening eagerly, her eyes shining, but Tony Chandler displayed not the slightest interest in the conversation. Much as Rosalie pitied Gloria, she shook her head and fell silent, refusing to go on with the time-wasting exchange. She had been through it all once and got nowhere. She was getting nowhere now.

What did occur to her was that it was all very odd. She had never before encountered such utter devotion of one so young to one so very old. Perhaps it was because Gloria, the last survivor of this proud family, dreaded the thought of being without a single relative in the world. Unless you counted her father's stepdaughter with whom she did not seem to be on the friendliest of terms, to say the very least.

But she had Tony, her future husband. Rosalie could see the great, winking stone of the ring on Gloria's finger, no brighter than the light in the girl's eyes when she looked at her fiance. Surely he would make up for a great many of the lacks in her life.

Rosalie was weary and physically uncomfortable by the time luncheon was over. Everything had been too heavy, too rich. There had been too many waits between courses due to Gloria's inexpert serving.

As she returned to the sickroom, she walked quickly past the door of the linen closet. She had almost—but not quite—managed to push out of her mind what had happened the night before. Now the memory of it came flooding back and her throat seemed to close over and she could feel a resurgence of the panic that had overwhelmed her.

When she came to the worn spot in the carpet, she almost caught her heel in it again and just in time, managed to skirt it without disaster. She stopped there and examined the frayed place with a frown.

It was odd, she mused. In this place that had certain evidences of luxurious living, there were also evidences of shabbiness and neglect. The worn carpet. The scanty supply of linens. The poor furnishings of the rooms she had looked into the night before.

And yet the luncheon had skimped nothing in the way of good food. There had been filet mignon steaks in mushroom sauce and artichokes and expensive wine and out-of-season strawberries in thick cream. Too, everything had been served on Spode china and the tablecloth had been of delicate lace and the silver had gleamed with the luster of many polishings. There had been a centerpiece of fresh flowers.

It was one more puzzling aspect of this strange, old place that was beginning to disturb Rosalie more and more.

Her patient had slept through the morning hours and Rosalie had not wanted to disturb her to administer her morning care. But now she was awake, her faded eyes staring but not moving when her nurse came into the room.

Rosalie tried to establish some line of communication between them. She stood close to the old woman and said, "I'm Rosalie Dexter. You've been sleeping most of the time since I came. I'm here to take care of you, Mrs. Aldrich. If there's anything you want, any way I can make you more comfortable, please try to let me know. Now I'm going to bathe you and change your nightgown. The bed wasn't changed last night. I meant to do it but something—something came up and prevented me. I'll do it now."

There was no answer, not even a flicker of the eyelids. Zena Aldrich was slipping rapidly out of her present world, seemed to have lost interest in everything it contained.

Rosalie went to the linen closet, propped the door open carefully and snatched at the linens she needed. She got a basin full of hot water from the bathroom down the hall and brought it back. Then she began the washing process.

As she bathed Mrs. Aldrich's face, she pushed the thin white hair off the wrinkled-webbed forehead. And stopped abruptly with the wash cloth half-raised. For she had come upon a scar high in the center of the forehead, an old, puckered scar in the shape of a crescent moon.

It was so old, so lost in the wrinkles, that it was difficult to identify it, but it looked very much like the scar of a burn. And Rosalie wondered what sort of accident Zena Aldrich had had, many years ago, to leave this memento.

3

SHE MEANT to mention the scar to Doctor Sargent (she hadn't been this silly as a schoolgirl, she acknowledged—bringing him into all her little everyday happenings, planning things to say to him at their next meeting) but she did not have any time with him alone that day.

Gloria came upstairs with him when he made his visit. She was chattering; there was no other word for it. Her light, rippling voice was like music and she was gazing earnestly into his face.

". . . do everything we can to help Miss Dexter and make things easier for her," she was saying. "That's why I've decided that she and I should change rooms. She can have the one next door, so that she'll be closer to Grandma, and I'll take the one upstairs. That will be better all around, don't you think?"

She paused to look anxiously from one to the other. She did not give Rosalie a chance to say anything at all but went on brightly, "I'll help you make the switch, Miss Dexter."

The doctor said, without seeming to show much interest, "I guess that's a good idea. Save her running back and forth over the stairs." Then he added, with a sudden grin, "And there'll be less chance of her being chased by bogie men."

Rosalie felt the hated warmth in her cheeks

and the blushing added to her humiliation. She bit back a sharp retort as she glared at him for she saw that he was not looking at her. His eyebrows were raised over Gloria's blank expression. "You haven't heard about Miss Dexter's little episode in the linen closet last night?"

There was nothing for Rosalie to do then except explain. Gloria made little cooing murmurs of commiseration and at the end of the account said, "But of course it must have been an accident! Who would possibly. . . ? Unless, of course, Jug. He's not—not quite bright, you know. Azie would deny it ferociously, because she would not allow any aspersions on her son, but the truth is he's feeble-minded, like a child really. This may have been his idea of a prank. I'll—I'll speak to him, Miss Dexter. I promise I will, and nothing like this will happen again. We don't want to lose another nurse, do we, Doctor?"

"Another?" Rosalie turned her head to look inquiringly at him. "Another nurse?"

"There were a couple before you," Gloria explained. "They did not stay very long. They said that Jug—frightened them. And that Azie was insolent and refused to wait on them. And one of them said," and she laughed a tinkling laugh, "that the house scared her, that it was strange and spooky."

"Twittering females," Doctor Sargent said contemptuously, and Rosalie, who had been entertaining thoughts of her own about taking herself off the case, blushed again.

It was undoubtedly true that the housekeeper was uncooperative because that afternoon it was

Rosalie and Gloria who made the change of bedrooms. Azie, Gloria said, had declared she had too much to do when asked to help.

"No matter, we can do it ourselves." There was an oddly stubborn streak in this soft-spoken girl. She shook her head when Rosalie suggested putting off the move for another day. "We might as well take care of it ourselves."

It took little time and effort to bring Rosalie's things from upstairs. But Gloria had racks and racks full of clothing, and she insisted that they all be moved up to the room on the third floor. Cosmetics, underwear, accessories all went, too, and Rosalie interpreted this as more evidence that Gloria was clinging to the delusion that her great-grandmother was going to live on for a long time.

I ought to straighten her out once and for all, she thought, force her to accept the truth. The shock will be too great for her if she won't let herself be prepared.

But when the change had been made, when Gloria was perched on the bed that had been hers and was now, temporarily, Rosalie's, she spoke of other things besides illness and death. She spoke of how lonely it sometimes was in the big house. Today, for instance, Tony and Julie had gone out on his boat.

"They're real water buffs. Although she got all this enthusiastic only recently—since she met him, in fact. I'm not as crazy about boating as I should be, seeing that Tony and I are going to be married. And Azie and Jug have gone to the village for groceries. Not that they'd be any companionship." A little shadow of something—fear?—had come into her eyes. Whatever it was, she turned her face away and her profile looked calm and clearly cut. "So I'm glad you're here, Rosalie. I hope you don't mind my calling you that. I am glad that Doctor Sargent asked the registry specially to have you on the case."

"He did? He really asked for me?" The words came out in a mindless burst and she knew that Gloria had heard the soaring notes in her voice because she laughed and turned her head back in Rosalie's direction.

"He did indeed. Why? Is that so surprising? He said you were a good nurse, the best private duty nurse on the lists. You should be flattered. He's an excellent doctor. And very attractive, too," Gloria teased. "If I didn't have all my attention wrapped up in Tony, I might make a try for the good doctor myself."

Rosalie couldn't think of anything to say. A crumb. That's all it was, a crumb. She didn't want to think that she was so hungry she could make a whole meal of it and she tried to change the subject.

But it wasn't easy with someone she had known for such a short time. Finally she seized upon the coming wedding, asked Gloria when it was to take place.

"In two weeks," Gloria told her. "Regardless of anything. It will be very quiet, of course, because of Grandma. But we've decided to go ahead with it anyway. Maybe that seems heartless but that's the way it's going to be," and again there was the hardness of steel in her voice.

After that there did not seem to be any topics of

conversation. They had no common meeting ground and only one mutual friend. And there wasn't much of anything more to say about Hugo Bannister. This time it was Gloria who mentioned the book he had been writing.

"He and my father were great friends. They were to have collaborated on the book, I believe. I came across, just a little while ago, some papers Daddy left. That's how I knew. After he died, Hugo decided to go it alone."

The conversation, with nothing to feed it, flickered out. Gloria wandered to the dressing table and sat there looking at herself critically. Her reflection seemed to reassure her and for a while she was thoughtful, seeming far away in some remote world of her own.

Perhaps, Rosalie guessed, she was thinking about Tony, seeing him and her stepsister alone in his boat and, knowing that the other girl was in love with him, worrying a little. Thinking about the wedding.

Rosalie wondered what type of ceremony it would be. In two weeks Zena Aldrich would undoubtedly be dead, but Gloria might be clinging to her belief that her great-grandmother would still be alive then and planning to be married right next door in the sickroom.

At any rate, it was not going to be a traditional sort of wedding. Rosalie had seen no white gown nor filmy veil among the things she had helped carry upstairs that afternoon. Gloria was not in the whirl of shopping and fitting and preparations of a bride-to-be as the day of her wedding approached.

Nor was Tony Chandler, she thought with a rush of pity for his fiancée, the typical impatient bridegroom. Here he was off spending the warm autumn afternoon with another girl, nor was he above trying to promote a flirtation with a nurse.

Well, let's face it, Rosalie said to herself, the whole place is nutty. She could sympathize with the nurses who had taken themselves off the case.

When she was alone again with her patient, Gloria having wandered off disconsolately to wait for Tony, the thick silence of the sickroom began to oppress her. The only sound was that of Mrs. Aldrich's shallow breathing. Even the ocean was hushed this afternoon. Rosalie felt as though she had been dropped into a great vacuum of stillness and, for no definite reason, something cold seemed to crawl along her nerves.

You got cabin fever after a while on these twenty-four hour, private duty cases. There were too many long, idle hours, too much of the same surroundings, too much solitude. You couldn't stand too much of it without getting what she called "the willies" and she knew that it was time now for her to get away from the sickroom for a little while.

She went to her patient and checked the vital signs. It was plain that Mrs. Aldrich's condition would not change for some time and that, once asleep, she would remain asleep for the rest of the afternoon; long enough, at any rate, for Rosalie to go out and get a breath of fresh air before she was needed again.

There was a thick sweater in a dresser drawer in her new room and she went and got it and fastened it around her shoulders. Walking very quietly, she went along the hall, down the stairs and out the front door. She had no idea, when she realized how stealthy she was being, why she was tiptoeing. Certainly no one would have raised any questions about her being entitled to a short respite from her duties. It was just something about this house. Secrecy begat secrecy. Wariness was born of uneasiness.

Last night, when she had arrived in the darkness, Rosalie hadn't been able to see much of the grounds. Now she saw everything: ugly, stunted pines; a few towering trees with trunks like sleeping serpents; the narrow path of pressed clam shells that led back to the village; the ragged cliffs that dropped down to the ocean.

The house stood almost at the edge of the rocky point of land. There was water on three sides of it and today the water scarcely moved. The last faint colors of the sunset were fading on the horizon. But there was no beauty there for when the sky darkened night would come suddenly and with it a return of whatever dangers the old house held.

Rosalie stood with her arms clasped around her body tightly, but the embrace did not stop her shivering. Dangers. She had not used that word in her mind before, but now she was certain that there was something menacing behind the red-tinted windows of the house. The glow of the sunset made them look as though they reflected the flames of a fire and she stood and looked at them, fascinated. And the shivering went on and on.

Another one of those twittering females, Doctor Sargent would have called her. Affected by an old house with glowing, red windows, the gathering dusk, the loud fluttering of her own nameless fears. Well, she would not give in to them. She would not run back inside like some timid spinster seeing ghosts in the shadows.

She followed a little path that led around to the back of the house and there came upon a barn, smaller than the house, of course, but gray-shingled like it and with the same sort of ornate carvings around its eaves. Her car, Rosalie remembered, should be there for there was no other garage in sight. This little building had undoubtedly been a coach house in the days of horses and carriages.

She'd had a flat tire and the tire might have been—but probably was not—repaired by Jug. She would go into the coach house and see. It would keep her out of the house for a little while longer and give purpose to her expedition outside.

There were no ground clam shells on this narrow foot path, only brown pine needles and small twigs that had blown across it. They made little crackling noises as she stepped on them. A gust of wind blew up suddenly and rattled the small bushes that bordered the path. The sun was gone now and the twilight seemed to come in from the sea and creep along behind her.

She began to run and she reached the coach house and a huge door stood gaping open, and she ran through it. Inside there was nothing but gloom, only faint light from the narrow windows on two of its walls.

When her eyes became used to the near darkness, she could see the outlines of her small car.

It was sandwiched in between a gleaming white sports car (which, she thought, belonged either to Gloria or Julie) and a great, hulking, onyx-black limousine that looked like a relic from the days of grandeur in motoring.

She could not see the tire that had been flat because the cars on either side of hers hid it from view. And so she went further into the barn.

And then she felt it. She felt the presence behind her. She was frozen for an instant, forced herself to move but was immediately thrown off balance by something thick and warm falling down over her head.

She began to choke and sputter for the thing that imprisoned her head and face smelled vile, like an old, decaying piece of fur. A lap robe. The thought came into her mind in that moment of panic, was washed away almost immediately in a surge of pure terror.

For the thing over her head was being drawn tighter and tighter, and she felt through its softness the biting of something drawn across her throat. The piece of fur, lap robe, whatever it was, was being tied with a piece of cord or rope, and it was being pulled so that it cut off her breathing.

She lifted her hands and clawed at the rope. She closed her fingers over it and she tried to tug it away. But the rotten stench of the thing wrapped around her head was clogging her nose and her throat, and she felt wave after wave of nausea churning and rising from her stomach. Her knees buckled and she sank, sick and suffocating, to the floor.

4

THERE WAS no time for a life-and-death struggle. This was not like the linen closet where extinction would have come with insidious slowness. If she were to survive rapid oblivion and instant demise, seconds counted.

By instinct only, because her brain seemed to be exploding, Rosalie thrashed about on the floor of the carriage house and when she wrenched her head from one side to the other, she felt the cord around her neck begin to loosen. Her hands seemed nerveless but she found she could lift them and grasp at the reeking thing that covered her. As she fought her way out of it, her lungs swelled and ached. By the time her face and then her head were free, she was weak and sobbing. She let herself drop back to the floor and lay there, shuddering.

Her mind began to clear. She knew that she could not remain there. Whoever had followed her out of the house, into the shadowy barn, crafty with a murderous purpose, might still be lurking about close at hand, ready to strike again now that the first attempt had proved unsuccessful.

She forced herself to stifle her ragged breathing, and quietly, so that no one outside the coach house would be able to hear a sound from inside it, she crawled forward on her hands and knees until she reached the place where her small car was squeezed in between the two larger ones.

What she had in mind was to obtain a tool, anything she could use as a weapon, from the trunk. But she remembered, panic striking her suddenly, that she had left the keys in the ignition when she had abandoned the car. She had given instructions to Jug about moving the car off the road. Suppose, having done as he was told, he had put the keys in his pocket! There was a better-than-even chance that that's where they were now.

They were not. They were there in the ignition; she could see their faint shine when she dragged herself up by the door handle and peered inside. She pulled open the door, snatched at the keys, slid around to the trunk and unlocked it. A few tools lay on its floor and from them she selected a jack handle.

Strength and confidence came back to her. At least she had something with which to defend herself. She would not be, as she had been twice before, a helpless victim for whoever was determined to kill her.

Why? The question throbbed in her brain over and over again as she made her way cautiously out of the barn and along the footpath that separated it from the house.

Why should anyone in this big, strange, ugly place want her out of the way? What had she done that she should be marked for death?

The light of the sunset was gone now and the dusk had thickened almost to darkness. The outlines of Moontide loomed in the fading light. It seemed to have grown in size, to rise even higher in the twilight, and there was a look of fearsomeness about its great, staring windows, dull and colorless now. Who in it spelled for her menace and danger?

She had no answer. She had come to Moontide in her capacity as a nurse. She happened to be here because, according to what Gloria had told her, Doctor Sargent had specifically asked to have her on the case.

That, too, was unexplainable. Why had he asked the registry to send her here and then scarcely said a civil word to her on the two occasions they had met?

Richard Sargent was in her thoughts for more than that one reason as she made her fear-filled journey back to the house. The tide was coming in noisily: the sound of the sea was almost like a human voice muttering angrily. It would have drowned any other sounds. She would not have heard anyone who might have crept up behind her, and she kept whirling around to make sure that there in the gathering darkness she was not being followed.

The reason her mind was occupied with Richard Sargent was because it was her intention, the moment she could reach a telephone, to resign from the case. Enough was enough. It would be sheer idiocy to remain here where murder had stalked her twice. So all right, let Gloria talk about the "pranks" of a man whose mind had reached the boyhood stage and developed no further.

Let Richard sneer at her supposed fancies and shrug about "accidents." She knew these two attempts had been something more sinister than pranks or accidents, and she was getting out just as soon as she could notify Doctor Sargent.

No one followed her. She reached the house without incident. When she got inside, she began to hunt for a telephone. There was none in the sickroom nor could she remember having seen one anywhere upstairs. The door of a small room off the hall was open, she peered into that and saw that it was evidently used as a telephone room. The instrument was on a table, there was a bench that ran along beside the table, the door could be closed for complete privacy.

A short list of names and telephone numbers was tacked on the wall. Rosalie found Doctor Sargent's and called it. She knew that he would not answer personally but she was a little disappointed when she reached only the answering service.

Doctor Sargent, she was told, was making house calls. Yes, Mrs. Aldrich was on his list of patients to be visited that night. He would undoubtedly be there before long. Was it an emergency? Did she wish to leave a message?

No emergency and no message. This was something she had to say to Richard personally. And having said it and taken herself out of this massive monster of a house, would she ever see him again?

You will have to get over this nonsense, my girl, she told herself. Why should you be seeing him again, except by chance? So let us have no more moping and mooning. Let's get with the program!

She opened the door and started out of the

room and then stopped short. From a room diagonally across the hall—a back parlor, she thought, because of its position—she heard voices. There were two distinctly different ones, both feminine, and both raised over their normal tones. Neither woman was making an effort to keep from being heard. Either that or both of them were caught up in such a bitter quarrel that they did not realize they were close to shrieking.

Because of the out-of-the-ordinary shrillness of the voices, Rosalie could not, at first, identify them. And then while she waited there until the quarrel had ended and they had moved on, so that she would not embarrass the owners of the voices, she came to realize that the participants in the heated exchange were Gloria Aldrich and Julie Merrick.

"You would not say things like this to me if Tony could hear you!" This was Gloria crying out in querulous little spurts.

Julie sounded calmer although there was something in her tones, something hard and vicious, that made Rosalie shiver. "You are so right, my darling step-sister! It's the image, you know. Do you know how he sees me? He thinks I'm 'sweet'! He told me that just a little while ago when we were out on his boat. So I can't disillusion him, now can I? I have to go on letting him see how sweet I am."

Her laugh was a disagreeable sound and then, following on its heels, was a shout. "But I will tell you, dear Gloria! You will never marry him—never! I love him the way I never dreamed possible, and I could make him love me if I had the chance. If I could get you out of the picture.

"And I will . . . I will!"

There was so much that was malevolent, so much that was menacing in what was being cried out that Rosalie felt a deep, sudden chill, like a blast of cold air, freeze her skin. Then there was a moment of silence. Julie's words seemed to hang on the air, echoing and ugly.

When she spoke again, it was in such an ordinary, flat-toned voice that what she was saying seemed even more horrible. "I will not let it happen. You will never marry him. There is only one way I can stop you and I shall take that means if I have to. I am only waiting for the right moment."

Rosalie heard Gloria's sharp intake of breath, like a terrified whimper, and then the rushing of footsteps. Then there was another set of footfalls. She waited until they died away, then peered out. When she reached the staircase, she looked up and saw Julie standing at the landing, her face in profile. Julie turned and looked down and the eyes of the two girls met.

Gloria's step-sister had not had time to rearrange her features. There was still on them a look of raging fury. Her eyes were glittering and her mouth was distorted.

At luncheon Julie had seemed serene and lovely, her face tranquil, her lips curving and sweet. Rosalie wondered why she had considered this girl even pretty. Now she was seeing cruelty in that face above her, the stamp of some evil purpose.

They stood glaring at each other and Julie made

no effort to hide the hostility that came pouring down, like something vile, onto the girl on the steps below her. Perhaps she was remembering, Rosalie thought with malaise creeping inside her, that the man she loved had let his fancy stray in this direction, too; that here was another potential rival for his affections.

In that moment, Julie looked as though she could kill.

Perhaps she had tried. Twice. Rosalie felt as though she had been set on fire. Her throat, her eyelids, her insides—all seemed to be aflame with the realization that she might be staring up into the face of her enemy.

Then she drew a long breath as her good sense came back. She remembered that she had not even met Julie last night when she had been locked into the linen closet. If Julie had seen Tony waging his little campaign, she must also have seen Rosalie's subtle rejection of his advances.

If anyone was in danger from Julie Merrick, it was Gloria.

That thought hung in Rosalie's brain when Julie turned, finally, with a little snort, and went up the rest of the stairs. It remained and grew to larger, stronger proportions when she came upon Gloria huddled inside the door of the sickroom.

Gloria's face was pale, more clay-colored than white. Her eyes were enormous and they were glazed with fright. She looked at Rosalie but did not seem to see her. She stood pressed against the wall, encased with a paralysis of fear.

When Rosaile spoke to her, asked if she could get her anything—a pill, a drink, a cup of coffee—

Gloria did not answer. She moved her body like someone sleep-walking and went out of the room, turned with a jerk and walked stiffly down the corridor.

Rosalie wanted to run after her, to take that rigid little body into her arms and console the girl as best she could. She resisted the impulse. There was nothing she could do for Gloria who was evidently in some sort of shock which might not wear off for a long time yet.

Besides, there was no way Rosalie could reassure her. She could not say convincingly, "You have no reason to be afraid," because that would be a lie. There was much to be afraid of; Rosalie was still shaken by her own experience in the carriage house. If she tried to talk to Gloria now, she might only impart to the other girl some of her own terror.

She went back to the bedroom. Mrs. Aldrich had evidently not stirred during her absence. Azie had been sitting by the bedside. Rosalie had not noticed her before in her concern for Gloria. Now the old woman got up and gave the nurse a single glance through the heavy lenses of her glasses. Rosalie thought she detected something accusing in it. Azie might believe that her mistress was being neglected so Rosalie said, to reassure her, "I just went outside for a breath of fresh air. I did not intend to stay so long."

Azie muttered, "You tell when you go."

"Next time I will. I promise."

A little while after Azie left the room, Gloria came back into it. She did not speak a word of greeting, merely went to her great-grandmother and then crossed the room and sat down on a chair there. Her face was still without color and she clasped and unclasped her hands in her lap. She looked like a frightened child. Rosalie went over to her and asked, "Can I get you anything, Miss Aldrich? Is there anything I can do for you?"

Gloria shook her head mutely so Rosalie left her there, knowing that she only wanted to be with someone, was afraid of being alone. Was afraid, perhaps, of another encounter with Julie.

Then why, Rosalie wondered, didn't Gloria insist that Julie leave the house? She had that right, certainly. Soon everything—the house, the estate, whatever Zena Aldrich owned—would belong to her. Julie could have no legal claim to any of it since she was not even related to Mrs. Aldrich.

But Rosalie could not imagine this gentle-mannered girl turning anyone out, not even the step-sister who had predatory designs on the man they both loved and who had gone so far as to threaten her. Gloria's softness of nature was evidently making her helpless and vulnerable against the ominous forces abroad in this big, dismal place.

Before long, Rosalie made another attempt to get Gloria to speak. It was not good for her, she knew, to remain locked too long in that near-catatonic state. If anything could bring her out of it, it might be a mention of Tony.

"Your fiance isn't coming tonight?"

The eyes lost their glassiness and took on a faint glow. The pale hands stopped torturing each other. "No, there is a meeting of the board of directors at the Yacht Club." It was little more than a whisper at first and then suddenly she burst out, "Oh, I shall be so glad when we are married at last! I can scarcely wait!"

She lapsed back into silence and sat without moving. She was still there when Doctor Sargent came. Hating to disturb her, Rosalie said gently, "I am sorry but I must speak to the doctor alone."

Gloria got up from her chair, smiled dimly at him and then left the room obediently.

Rosalie turned to face Doctor Sargent. As his eyes traveled over her, she remembered that she had done nothing to improve her appearance except wash her hands since she had returned to the house. Her uniform had become wrinkled during her struggle to free herself from the lap robe, her hair must be untidy and streaming.

Just once, she thought, I would like to look professional and calm and neat when he looks at me.

She began to speak quickly to explain the dirty and wrinkled skirt, her touseled hair, the run in one of her nylons. "I didn't want to take time to change." Then she told him about going into the coach house to look at her car, how she had been attacked, had come close to death.

"Again," she said. "Once more. And don't bother to tell me that it did not happen or that the poor, dim-witted manservant was playing games. Or that I am."

Because recounting it brought back all the horror and because she was so agitated that everything in her mind rushed out in a burst of candor, she blurted, "If you've got any funny ideas, forget them, Doctor Sargent! I'm sure there must be hordes of women who dream up false symptoms and act out little dramas to make you notice them. You can be sure—oh, you can be very sure indeed—that this isn't something like that!"

She saw his face grow dark with a flush. He stabbed her with his glare. "What a conceited ass you must think I am! I had no such thoughts. I just find all this hard to believe, that's all. You can't actually be convinced that there is something around here who's trying to kill you?"

"I can and I am, and that's why I'm leaving just as soon as you can get another nurse for this case. You can call the registry or I will if you prefer. Perhaps there is someone in particular you want this time, too."

He went on staring at her. "Just what is that supposed to mean?"

"That I don't understand why you did—ask for me, I mean. I never worked on a case with you before. You didn't know me all that well."

"But I . . . Rosalie, look . . ."

He had begun to speak but he stopped abruptly, concerned about what was happening to her. Everything seemed suddenly to have caught up with her, a delayed reaction. A little whirl of dizziness spun her senses around and she was momentarily blinded. She did not consciously reach out for him but when her brain cleared, she found that she was clinging to him.

"I seem always to be grabbing . . ."

She, too, broke off, the words dying in her throat. Because he had stepped closer to her. Her face was only inches away from his coat. She could smell his shaving lotion mingled with an antiseptic solution. It was wonderful. It was mind-numbing. She wanted to remain right there, to drop her cheek against the hardness of his chest and feel the strength of his arms around her.

It would have been enough at first. But then she had to raise her face for she was helpless against the overwhelming need to put her mouth against his. His head was bent toward her and she drew it down even closer; and then their lips were together and the warmth went sweeping over her until she was mindless with it.

With her hands pressing against the back of his neck, she could feel the short, bristly hair there, her fingertips throbbing. She began to murmur something against the hardness of his mouth.

He released her, his arms falling away while hers still held him, his lips drawing away as he lifted his head. She stood swaying and then came back with a jolting wrench to the reality of the sickroom. The lovely warmth she had felt was replaced by the hot fire of shame.

She stared at him in horror, knowing that she was the one who had made the embrace happen, had kissed with the greater fervor; it was she who had held him imprisoned in her arms for the longer time.

Appalled, she tried to speak and her voice came out in a croak. She said inanely, "Oh, I am so sorry! It was—oh, I don't know!"

His voice, too, sounded unnatural. "We both know why it happened. You were upset, Rosalie. Unhappy. We tend to reach out and like the man and the mountain, I was there."

He was making things worse. He was making excuses for her. He was so embarrassed for her that he was seizing at anything to explain away her shameful behavior. If he had spoken differently, if he had apologized for himself instead of for her, if he had said one word of tenderness, she might have been able to bear it. As it was, she never wanted to look at this man's face again.

When she turned away, he said tentatively, "Rosalie?" and at the inquiring note in his voice, she stiffened with outrage.

Did he think she would return to him for more meaningless love-making? Or did he believe, as he was entirely justified in believing, that she had given him a signal and that he could expect something more than a few moments of hugging and kissing in the presence of a patient?

She was fiery with anger, not at him because he was, after all, a man and she had acted like some cheap and ready thing, forgetting her professionalism, her stature as a nurse.

"Rosalie?"

"Forget it!" she gritted. "Put me down as another neurotic female. It's a new role for me. This house . . . what has happened to me here . . . Doctor Sargent, will you kindly make arrangements to have me relieved as soon as possible?"

She left him there and went into the room next door and closed herself into it. Her heart was still racing so heavily that she could feel its hurt. She ignored it and began to snatch at the clothing hanging in the closet. She threw them on the bed but before she had a chance to open her suitcase, there was a knock on the door.

Because she thought Richard had come to make another attempt to speak to her, she drew herself up and settled her features into a mask of composure before she walked to the door and threw it open. She felt at a loss when she found herself facing Gloria.

There was someone downstairs waiting to talk to her, Gloria told her. She added, when Rosalie's eyebrows raised in inquiry, that it was Sheriff Wellman, the head of Stoneport's small police force.

"What in the world . . . ?"

"He didn't say," Gloria interrupted. "Just that he wanted to speak to you."

Rosalie thought that perhaps Doctor Sargent had, after all, reported the first attempt on her life. There would not have been time for him to summon the sheriff about the second one. It had been only moments since she had told him about that.

She took time to smooth her hair and make an attempt to brush off the skirt of her uniform. In the back parlor where the sheriff waited, she learned that it was not about herself that he had come. It was about someone who was already dead.

That was how she learned that Hugo Bannister, that kindly, unassuming little man who had been her patient, had not died of a heart attack after all but had been murdered.

5

SHERIFF WELLMAN said: "The relatives came to claim the body, you see. There hadn't been any question of an autopsy. Old Doc Mason had seen Bannister only the day before he died. But you know that. You were there when he came."

She was still trying to absorb what he had told her. She did not notice, at first, the long stretch of silence that fell into the little room where he was interviewing her.

"In here," he had said, motioning to the door of the back parlor. "Seems to be the only place down here where we won't have to shout at each other."

So they sat facing each other, she on a love seat of maroon plush with arms and back of pale, carved walnut, and he on a chair of faded green velvet.

The other furnishings, too, had the look of age: a marble-topped table, an old-fashioned phonograph with a horn like a huge morning glory, an oversized ottoman. The room was crowded and cluttered for in addition to the furniture there were a number of cabinets and hanging shelves full of figurines carved of what looked like jade, and some of ivory, and scrimshaw articles—the paper cutters and miniature anchors and crosses and beads of whalebone that sailors used to fashion during long whaling voyages.

On the fireplace mantle was an elaborate ship model that she had noticed, in passing, when she came into the room. Most of her mind was occupied with the sheriff's shocking news.

She grew aware of the silence and was confused as to whether or not he had asked a question and was waiting for an answer.

She said, "I'm sorry. I'm afraid I didn't hear the last part of it."

"The family," he repeated. "They flew in from the West Coast this morning. All he had was a niece and nephew. I don't think he saw them very often because, with his bad heart, traveling was out for him. But they evidently corresponded quite a bit because the woman got a letter from him only last week.

"Haven't got it with me, of course. It's locked up back at the office."

She sat staring at him, waiting for him to go on. He was not at all what Rosalie would have expected an officer of the law to be like. He was not very tall and he had a long, slender face and a delicate mouth that drooped and gave him a doleful look. His hair was turning from blond to gray, and everything about him—skin, eyes, hair—was pale. With her nurse's critical eye, she thought he looked frail, not nearly strong enough for the vigorous life he would have to lead.

But his voice sounded strong and authoritative enough.

"Locked up," he said, "for safekeeping. But I can tell you, almost word for word, what was in it. Bannister wrote to his niece that the book he had been writing was almost finished. And that he already had a publisher interested in it."

His forehead crumbled as he made an effort to quote the letter accurately.

"What he wrote was, 'The publication of my book will cause certain people some embarrassment, I'm afraid, but I'm going ahead with it anyway. In spite of everything. In spite of threats and the fact that somebody may try to kill me to keep certain secrets from coming to light.'"

Rosalie put in, "But certainly he didn't think . . . ! Oh, no, he wasn't afraid or anything like that!"

"You know that for sure? Remember, he had that bad heart and couldn't live for so much longer, anyway. That'd make a man careless about certain things, wouldn't it? That's what I wanted to ask you. What were those certain things? What was in that book he was writing? What was in it that somebody couldn't bear for it to be published? Come on, Miss Dexter, you were his nurse. Patients and nurses get very close, I hear. Being alone together so much, probably. He wouldn't have kept many things from you, now would he?"

She looked back at him levelly. "Yes, he would. I never saw any of his writing. He did all of it in bed, one of those hospital beds that has a pull-up table. And there was a bedside table with a drawer that he put his manuscript in and kept locked. But you must know that if you've examined the room. And seen the book? Read it? Then you don't need me or anyone else to tell you what was in it."

"There is no book."

"But you said . . ."

"I know what I said, Miss Dexter. That he had been writing a book we learned from his niece. And you've confirmed it. But where is it? There's the question. You're right about one thing. I have been all over that room, pried open the drawer. Searched the rest of the house, too. No book. We'll try again tomorrow." There was a hard glitter in his eyes. "But I got an idea that whoever killed him didn't want that book published and took it away and destroyed it.

"Were you," he asked with an abrupt change of subject, "the only one who took care of him?"

"I was his private duty nurse. I stayed in the house. But I usually went to bed at night when he actually did not need anyone with him all the time. There was a manservant who slept in the room next to his, Benjamin Choate, who would have heard him if he had called out and who would have summoned me if I had been needed."

The sheriff nodded. "Choate, yes. We've talked to him."

"I still cannot believe," she began.

"But somebody did," he interrupted. "Somebody fed Hugo Bannister poison. They did the post mortem this morning. The relatives insisted on it and we went to work and got the order. The report came in just a little while ago. Arsenic, that's what they found. Enough of it, the coroner said, to kill a dozen men."

She began to shake her head and went on shaking it steadily, as though there were some sort of mechanical device inside it over which she had no control.

"Who would kill him?" she whispered. "He was

an even-tempered, kindly man who would not have harmed anyone. Besides," and her voice grew stronger, "Doctor Mason attributed death to a cardiac vascular accident, a massive blow. That's the way he signed the certificate."

"Doc Mason," the sheriff said with a shrug, "is getting along in years. Can't blame him for the mistake if he was treating Bannister for a bad heart all along. Yep, Mason's getting old. Been passing over some of his cases to this young feller, this Doctor Sargent."

"I know." Rosalie's heart leaped absurdly at the sound of Richard's name. Then she forced composure upon herself and concentrated on trying to believe what the sheriff had told her. "A book! That doesn't seem to be enough cause for anyone to murder him. That's what you did say, wasn't it? Not an accident? He didn't. . . ? No, he wouldn't!"

She pushed the idea of suicide out of her mind. It was unthinkable when she remembered the zest for living, the lively inquisitiveness about all things, the drive and industry that kept him working on the book at the sacrifice of rest and sleep.

"He wouldn't. Of course not!"

"It was murder, that's for sure." Sheriff Wellman spoke through tight lips. "Never had a murder in Stoneport before. Got no facilities, lab, nothing like that. That's why I'm turning the whole thing over to the state police. They'll be coming along soon, Miss Dexter. They'll want to talk to you themselves. So you'll expect them. Stick around. Be available. They'll probably get around to you tomorrow."

"But I won't be here then!"

His eyes, so pale they were almost colorless, were cold and bright as they stared at her. "No? Not be here? Why's that?"

"Because I do not intend to spend another night in this house!"

She told him all the reasons. She went back to the moment of her arrival. She described how someone had pushed her into the linen closet, locked the door and left her to die.

"There's a servant here—Jug. He is not—well, not quite right in the head. Miss Aldrich—it is her great-grandmother who owns this place—said that Jug might be playing a prank. I couldn't quite make myself believe that. And then this afternoon," and her voice broke.

It took her a little while to get it all out but she finally managed to describe what had happened in the carriage house, how close she had come to being smothered to death.

"I don't go along with the idea that it was Jug being playful this time, either. I think I would have heard him if he had come up behind me. He sort of—sort of lumbers, and his footsteps are heavy. Besides, he could have choked me to death in a matter of seconds. He wouldn't have had to bother with an old lap robe and a piece of cord. His hands are big. He'd have had no trouble grabbing my throat with them, pressing the life out of it."

Her voice was labored and squeaky, exactly as though there were strong fingers around her neck at that very moment. Her own fingers laced and unlaced, and she was unaware of their movement. She forced herself to go on.

"And there is something about this house—oh, I don't know! It is so big and dark and—well, desolate. It is as though something tragic or evil had happened here that left an atmosphere still charged with it. Are old houses, do you think, affected by the things that go on under their roofs? Can you see and feel old sadnesses and crimes in places as you can in people who are tragedy-haunted?"

All her self-discipline seemed to have broken down and she knew that she was babbling, but she could not seem to stop. And while she had been speaking, pouring out all that idiocy, Sheriff Wellman's face had been changing. When she stopped at last, his features were cool and stiff; and he seemed to have withdrawn behind a mask and left only this expressionless facade before her.

Well, she thought, I have blown it. The sheriff was evidently literal-minded, a man who had faith only in facts and figures and no sympathy at all with mysticism. What she had done was make him uneasy and suspicious of her sanity.

Rosalie said, "But certainly it would be all right if I just went home? I live only a few miles from Stoneport, not far at all. If I leave my telephone number and address, wouldn't that be all right? I really don't have to remain right here on the premises, do I?"

The sheriff said firmly, "Lieutenant of the state police said you were to stay here. That means here. In this house." He bit on the words and, with a negating motion of his head, seemed to be hanging onto them. "You're a witness, Miss Dexter. And maybe something more than that."

He got up and pushed back the green velvet chair. She saw that he was finished, that he was intending to leave. She ran after him and seized him by the arm.

"What did you mean by that last remark?"

"Only that in cases like this you don't jump to the first conclusion. Sure, the book. That could be the motive but, on the other hand, it could be something else. The money, for instance. When you got money, you got greed. When you got greed, you maybe got somebody that'd kill for the money."

She could feel under the khaki sleeve the hardness and thinness of his arm bone. "Please don't go off without explaining all that to me. Tell me what you're talking about!"

"The will." His mouth wore a twist of cynicism. "Hugo Bannister was a rich man. You think that nephew and niece'd come flying three thousand miles and more if he was some poor old bum without a dime to his name? That house of his must be worth plenty. And there was the Bannister fortune, quite considerable at one time. Seems those relatives of his aren't going to get all of it, either.

"You see, Miss Dexter, Hugo Bannister's favorite occupation was writing. Not only that book but he wrote letters all the time. The niece, especially. She was the one who got the most of them. And in one of the last ones he sent, he mentioned you. Told about how much he'd come to like you and how he intended to leave you something when he died. We're waiting for a copy of the will now. When we get it and it turns out you're all of a sudden a rich woman—well, that's going to throw a different light on matters, isn't it?"

He actually seemed to become excited over the prospect. For the first time, she saw him smile. She tried to smile, too, over the idiocy of the idea. She would have given anything she owned to be able to laugh away the ridiculous theory he had just expounded. But there was a rising of icy spray inside her that washed away her conviction that he could not possibly have meant what he said, and it left only gathering terror.

Desperation made her inarticulate. There were other things she wanted to tell him: that earlier that evening, right here in this little room, there had been a bitter quarrel between the other two young women who lived in this house; and that one of them had threatened another in unmistakable language. But she could not remember now exactly what it was that Julie Merrick had said, nor describe her tone of voice, nor describe the look of murderous anger on Julie's face when she had seen her standing on the staircase landing. He would think such descriptions sprang from the same sort of fancies that made her babble about the atmosphere of the old house.

If she managed to make him listen to a recital of the quarrel, he wouldn't put much stock in that, either. He would doubtlessly minimize the whole thing, shrug it off as a "cat fight" between two jealous women.

When he reached the door, he turned and warned her again about leaving the premises. He must have seen something in her face—a bleakness, a shimmering of the fear that chilled her.

He said, "Miss Dexter, if you're thinking I should leave you protection here, I'm sorry but it just can't be done. I got three deputies, one for each shift. In the summer when there's more traffic, visitors, like that, I get a few college kids for the auxiliary force. But this time of year I got nobody to spare to hang around and watch the place. Kind of a losing proposition it'd be, anyhow, the big house, all the grounds around it. One man wouldn't be much good. You just take it easy. Keep on your guard. Stick to the sickroom and don't go wandering around."

He seemed to have softened a little, grown a bit more human, and his next question sounded like ordinary curiosity. "Who is it that's sick, the old lady?"

It seemed odd to Rosalie that the news of Zena Aldrich's impending death had not reached the village. Remote as Moontide was, it housed a family so old and prominent that it should have been the object of the townspeople's interest.

Yet Rosalie could not remember ever reading anything about the Aldriches in the local newspaper. Perhaps the occupants of Moontide were isolated, cut off from the stream of living in the rest of the world. Azie and Jug would not have gossiped with the tradespeople in town. The doctors who had attended Mrs. Aldrich—first old Doctor Mason and recently, according to what she had learned, Richard Sargent—would not have discussed their patient with outsiders. So perhaps it was not so odd after all that the sheriff had not known of the woman's terminal illness.

"Mrs. Aldrich, yes," she said in answer to his question.

"Funny," he mused. "Here I have been living in the village all my life, close as it is to this place, and I never once laid eyes on her. Not many other people have, either, from what I hear. They're like hermits up here. Them two, the servants, come into the stores now and then. Him, he might be feeble-minded, but he drives the car all right. Never had to give him a traffic ticket. They never have anything to do with anybody, them two. Just get their supplies and off they go. Funny setup, this is. Young girl, the one that let me in, pretty as a picture but acts like you—scared of something, she seemed. Well, Miss Dexter, don't know as I blame you for having the heebie-jeebies. This is a spooky old place."

Thanks a lot for that, she thought, watching him open the door. Her apprehensions were stronger than ever now. It was all very well for him to tell her to be on her guard and stay close to the sickroom. To get there, she had to go up over the badly lighted staircase, walk the length of the shadowy hall. She saw it in her mind, all those long stretches of darkness in which there might be hidden more lurking danger than had yet overtaken her.

Phrases clamored in her brain. Two attempts. Two failures. Three times and out. Would her faceless enemy be luckier the next time? She could not bear it a moment longer in that small room with the ticking of the mantle clock and her own heavy heartbeats the only sounds.

Her hand outstretched, as though she could ward off the evil, she fled up to the second floor, her feet making swift, soft falls as she ran. The hushed stillness seemed even thicker up here and even more ominous.

Only a short distance from the door of Zena Aldrich's bedroom, she halted abruptly. She had heard other footsteps behind her. A long shadow fell across her path. She could not turn. Her feet were rooted, her throat too tight with its column of fear for her rising scream to come through it.

Arms reached out and wrapped themselves around her. A hand pressed over her mouth.

6

SHE WAS PULLED BACKWARD through an open door. She could feel her feet sliding over a strip of thin carpet, and she struggled to hold her balance while she fought to free herself from her captor.

Over the man's hand, she could see, her eyes wide and staring, that the room she was being dragged into was mottled with shadows from the hall light. And except for the sound of her scuffling and the breathing of the one who held her, it was deathly still.

Her lungs felt full and hot. Stunned with fear, she could barely lift her hands to the fingers that covered her mouth. But she managed to grasp at them and she pulled and they fell away. She heard someone laugh softly.

Then the bite of the hands was at her shoulders. She was spun around. She could see the man's face in a stream of light. It was Tony Chandler's and he went on chuckling as he looked down at her.

"Well, quite a little wildcat, aren't you?"

"Are you out of your mind?" The words burst furiously out of her sore mouth. "Where do you get the nerve? Just who do you think you are?"

"Somebody who believes in grabbing the golden opportunity when it comes along." His voice was light and mocking, but there was nothing jocular about the hot glow in his eyes. "Rosalie, sweetie, I had to do it this way. I knew I'd never get a chance to talk to you alone once you had closeted yourself in with the old woman."

She made an attempt to pull away. "Let me go. I should be with my patient."

He asked carelessly, "She's going to die anyway, isn't she? No, nursie dear, you're not getting away until you promise you'll meet me later. Life is for the living, baby. Gather rosebuds—you know?"

"I think you *are* out of your mind." She stared directly into his face, not wanting to let him see how badly he had frightened her nor how much his nearness and foolish prattle repelled her.

He laughed again and went on. "Beautiful, the minute I laid eyes on you I knew we could have something going. No, listen!" as she tried to hold herself away from him by stiffening her body. "It's true. We both know it, even if you're not ready to admit it yet. But that's all right. I like a girl who puts up a fight for a little while.

"Every one I've ever met," he said with a smug little smirk that revolted her, "has fallen into my arms like a ripe peach. Until now. Maybe that's why I'm panting for you, baby. You sat at the table with me at lunch today and you never gave me a tumble. I might have been that bonehead, Jug. Not a flicker, not a smile. But we'll make up for that now, won't we?"

"We will not!" She forced her voice to stay flat and even. "Mr. Chandler, this is ridiculous. Like some old movie on the late, late show. Come on, act your age. Take your hands off me and let me go."

His grip merely became stronger and for the

sake of saying something—anything—to divert him from his growing ardor, she said, "Gloria—Gloria told me that you weren't coming tonight."

"So you do keep track of me! Well, the meeting broke up early. So I thought I'd just amble over on the chance that I might find you alone. The front door was open and I heard you in the back parlor. Don't throw Gloria's name at me, baby doll. She's a wishy-washy specimen compared to you. I was right. From the fight you put up a few minutes ago, it's plain there's fire under that ice maiden exterior."

"You couldn't be more wrong!"

He bent his face closer to hers with a smile that was evidently meant to be devastating and she took advantage of that moment when he leaned forward to wrench her shoulders free. He went lunging ahead, off-balance, and she stepped back quickly out of his reach. In his efforts to keep himself from falling, he executed a few little quick-time steps, like an amateurish performer, and she could not keep herself from laughing at him. The assaults of rapidly changing emotions—fear and surprise and indignation—had brought her feelings close to the surface. Her laughter was almost hysterical.

The sound of it infuriated him. He regained his balance and turned and came toward her but she evaded him deftly and slipped through the door.

"You think this is the end of the story," he growled. "Not much, sweetie. No, not much."

And then, as she was passing the door of the room next to the one in which the absurd little scene had been played, she heard the soft click of a latch. She stopped, appalled.

Someone had been there then, only a few feet away, while Tony had been attempting to make love to her. Someone had stood in an open doorway and listened to what was going on in the other room. Someone was perhaps at this moment hearing again what had been said and, consumed with jealousy and perhaps murderous hatred, was fashioning evil plans in an inflamed brain.

Rosalie stood still for a moment, imagining that she could feel that flood of venom pouring over her. She wanted to cry out the truth to whoever was standing behind that locked door in torment.

She did not have the slightest personal interest in Tony Chandler. To her he was merely a nuisance—a spoiled, rich, emotionally immature boy who found irresistible whatever he could not obtain easily. He did not even know how to make love attractively, she thought, remembering with a lost wave of longing how Richard's arms had felt around her, how moved she had been by his kisses. No man had ever moved her in that way, and even if Tony Chandler had not belonged to another girl, he could never mean anything at all to her because he was not Richard Sargent.

Poor Gloria! Rosalie's heart was soft with pity when she remembered that Gloria was looking forward to a wedding in two weeks time with a man who was the poorest sort of husband material. Tony Chandler would undoubtedly always have a roving eye. The marriage wouldn't have a chance.

Rosalie hoped with all her heart that it had not been Gloria who had stood in the doorway of the room down the hall and heard that foolish, silent movie little drama. Better that it had been Julie Merrick, even though the thought of the dark-haired girl who could be serenely lovely one minute and a virago the next made Rosalie tense and uneasy. She could imagine those feelings of unreturned love festering in someone who seemed to have two distinct personalities. She knew the danger.

When she went into the sickroom, Rosalie immediately became a nurse again, everything forgotten but the needs of her patient. Even during the short time she had been at Moontide, Mrs. Aldrich seemed to have weakened. It was nothing more than an unsubstantiated impression because when she took vital signs, there was no appreciable change in them. The pulse was weak and slow. Blood pressure was 100 over 70. Her temperature was slightly below normal. None of it alarming, none of it unusual for an old woman in her condition.

Maybe, Rosalie said silently to her patient, you may make it to the wedding yet.

Although, of course, it would not matter much to her at all. She might not even be aware of what was going on around her, if they had the wedding performed here in this room, any more than she was aware now of the girl's presence in the room.

Rosalie touched her gently to awaken her for the bathing and turning processes, but most of all to see if she could spark some interest in living. Sometimes that helped. Perhaps by sheer will of spirit Mrs. Aldrich could survive until after her great-granddaughter's wedding.

Rosalie pushed the dry white hair back from the papery skin of the forehead. She saw again the crescent-shaped scar near the hairline, and she wondered about it once more. Then she found herself hoping that the accident that had caused it had not occurred as long ago as she guessed. She hoped that Zena Aldrich had not been so young that the marring of her beauty was a shatteringly important matter.

True, she might have hidden it by wearing bangs or a fringe of curls over it, but she might always have been conscious of it, fretted about it, grown shy and withdrawn because of it.

Sheriff Wellman had spoken about her hermit-like existence. Rosalie wondered if the woman had always closed herself into this big, desolate place or if, before her marriage, she had been gay, social-minded, life-loving.

She tried to imagine the young Zena, tried to picture her in a ball gown with tiny slippers on her feet, a fan in her hand. She must have been pretty because there were still faint, faded traces of beauty. The bones were good, those in her face high and well-formed. Her skin, before age had darkened it, had undoubtedly been a warm olive, and her eyes were still an attractive shade of brown. Yes, it was plain that Zena Aldrich had been a striking figure in her youth.

This is crazy, Rosalie thought, realizing suddenly what she was doing.

Here she was falling into the trap she swore she would avoid. She was becoming personally interested in a patient, feeling tenderness for that young girl who no longer existed, pitying her because her life was so nearly over. She had been determined, after Hugo Bannister, to remain detached and uninvolved.

That train of thought, bringing Hugo Bannister into her mind, did nothing to comfort her. She was seeing him now not as he had been when she had taken care of him but as a body with a lethal dose of poison inside it, a murder victim.

And because of that she, the most unlikely of all people, was forced to remain here in this house because she had been his nurse. A "witness," the sheriff had said. He had hinted that she was something more than that, that she was a possible suspect in the case.

It was not bad enough that she could feel this dreadful and oppressing atmosphere of menacing evil all around her. Now she had been put in double jeopardy; her life was in danger and there hung over her the threat of involvement in a murder investigation. She might even be arrested and arraigned and formally tried.

She would not let herself believe in the latter premise. Innocent people were quickly ascertained to be innocent. Yet try as she would, she could not banish the feeling that a tight net was weaving itself around her.

The night passed slowly. Mrs. Aldrich stirred several times and once she muttered something unintelligible. Rosalie bent close to her and asked, "Is there anything you want? Anything I can get you?" but when the woman opened her eyes, they were drug-glazed and she fell back to sleep immediately.

Afraid that her patient would awaken again and find herself alone. Rosalie remained beside the bed all night. She fell into a doze shortly before dawn and awoke a few hours later with her body aching. There were cramps in the back of her neck and her legs were stiff. She moved around the room to loosen her muscles and she began to develop a headache.

She wished that someone would come, Jug with coffee or Azie to relieve her so that she could bathe and change into a fresh uniform. And after a while someone did come, but it was not the old servant or her son but Gloria who did not look as though she had spent much of the night sleeping, either.

There were faint smudges of weariness under the girl's eyes and a sleep-walking look about her movements. She was, as always, impeccably dressed. This morning she had on a simply-cut frock of so pale a pink that it appeared almost white in the gloom of the sickroom.

And Gloria had done something to her hair, Rosalie saw. By means of some sort of rinse, she had lightened it so that it was almost the shade of Rosalie's own. Too, she had cut it and arranged it the way Rosalie wore hers. She had changed the color of her lipstick and when she stared at the other girl, Rosalie had the feeling that she was looking into a mirror.

She was struck again by the resemblance between them, more pronounced this morning since Gloria had changed the color and arrangement of her hair and used the same kind of makeup. There was no question in her mind. The transformation had to be deliberate. And when Rosalie realized the reason for the imitation, she was struck with pity.

She did not wonder now who had stood behind the door of the room down the hall and listened to Tony's attempts at lovemaking. It must have been Gloria who loved him without reason and whose heart must have broken when she heard him making advances to someone who was virtually a stranger.

Of course she was terrified of losing him. Learning that he was attracted to this older girl, she had doubtlessly tried to change her appearance, to make herself look as much like that girl as possible in order to rekindle his ardor.

It was, in Rosalie's opinion, touchingly pathetic. Especially in view of the fact that the effort Gloria had expended was senseless. It was not her looks that had roused Tony Chandler's interest. He was trying to promote something because she was a novelty, he had found her unattainable, he was bored.

How was she to tell Gloria that? She wanted to reassure the other girl, tell her that she had nothing at all to fear as far as she herself was concerned. But how exactly was she to say it? She couldn't come out bluntly with the news that she wouldn't have this character, whom Gloria loved so blindly, if he came gift-wrapped in thousand-dollar bills.

But she had no choice; odious as the task was, she had to do it.

7

SHE BEGAN, "Gloria, last night after I finished talking to the sheriff . . ."

Gloria broke in, "Oh, yes, I meant to ask you about that. What did he want with you?"

Rosalie hesitated. Should she or should she not? The circumstances of Hugo Bannister's death could not remain a secret for any length of time, of course, but she did not know whether or not she should be the one to reveal them to Gloria. The daughter of Hugo Bannister's friend had enough to distress her already.

As it turned out, Rosalie did not have to make the decision for Gloria did not wait for an answer. She seemed to forget everything except her great-grandmother as she went to the bedside and looked down at the old woman.

"She's a little better, don't you think? Have you seen any improvement?"

Rosalie wished that she could give this girl some small consolation, the repeating of even a few words from the dying old woman. But there was nothing to quote.

"She did rouse herself a little last night and she tried to say something."

"What? What was it?"

"Nothing specific. She merely mumbled. She

slept easily after that. And today, she is quiet, as you see."

"I want her to be alive when I am married." Gloria spoke in a breathless rush. There was a hint of tear shine in her eyes. "The ceremony will be right here in this room. I have told Tony it must be that way and he understands. All the arrangements have been made. I am going to marry him, you know. Nothing is going to stop that!"

Her voice had hardened and she stared levelly into the other girl's face. Rosalie had an uneasy moment when she feared that Gloria would burst out with an accusation, cry out that her great-grandmother's nurse was trying to take her fiance away from her.

"Of course nothing will. Gloria, I'm sure he loves you. Nothing—nobody will be able to stop that." It was all that she was able to say. She finished weakly, "In a couple of weeks, you will be Mrs. Tony Chandler."

Gloria dropped her head and her little choking sob sounded like grief over the sad little wedding ceremony to come.

A moment later she said, "I'll stay with her if you want to go down and get some breakfast. Jug said that his mother isn't feeling well this morning so we will all have to shift for ourselves. I had my coffee. What about her?" and she nodded toward the woman in the bed. "Can you get her to eat anything at all?"

"Liquids only. I'll try soup and fruit juice again today. I'll bring something up with me when I come. It will take me a little while. I've got to bathe and change."

She was used to moving rapidly, dressing quickly. It was not very much later that she went downstairs, feeling relaxed and clean in a fresh uniform. No one else seemed to be abroad in the house. The halls were deserted and there were no sounds from any of the rooms that she passed.

The door to the drawing room on the first floor was open and Rosalie saw, when she looked into it, that it was empty. She had never been in this room and had merely glimpsed a portion of it in passing. Now she went to the threshold, curious about it, interested in it because last night she had been wondering how the young Zena had spent her time. Had this room ever been used for parties, for entertaining, even for the ordinary pursuits of everyday living?

Had Zena, the daughter of the house, sat here with suitors, played for them on the huge, dully-gleaming grand piano that stood in one corner? Had the rugs ever been rolled up and the furniture pushed back so that she and her friends could dance?

It did not seem likely. The room had an air of austerity which did not lend itself to light-hearted chatter and music and dancing. Rosalie felt that it always must have been like this, forbidding and formal with dark, heavy chairs and divans, maroon velvet draperies pulled across tall windows, massive fireplace of white marble with the wonderfully colored Chinese vases on its mantle.

A portrait hung over this mantle and Rosalie went further into the room and crossed it to study at closer range the subject of the portrait and to read the nameplate at its base.

It read: EZRA THAYER, 1815–1899.

The man was dressed in the uniform of a sea captain. He had stern features, an oversized nose and wiry eyebrows and a squarish jaw. A curly beard bristled from his chin but it did not hide his mouth, which was thin and cruel.

Rosalie studied the portrait with interest. She knew that she was looking into a reproduction of the face of the man who had built this ugly, desolate place and lived in it during the latter years of his life. This was Zena Aldrich's father, but Rosalie could not see anywhere at all in the portrait any resemblance to the old lady who lay upstairs dying.

People changed with years and sickness, yet there should have been something about this man that he had passed down to his daughter. It was unusual. Rosalie had noticed that girl children tended to look more like their fathers than their mothers. Undoubtedly this had not been true in this case.

She looked around to see if there was a portrait of Zena's mother, wanting to see what the woman that Captain Thayer had married looked like, if Zena had, in fact, resembled her. There was none anywhere in sight.

There was a standing photograph on the grand piano but that, Rosalie decided immediately, had been taken of Zena in her youth. The clothing—a high, ruffled neckline, tucked bodice, ballooning sleeves—belonged to the late nineties or possibly the turn of the century. The picture might have been taken, and undoubtedly was, just before the death of Zena's father.

The photograph was not full length, but cut off at the waist, and it showed her dark hair in curls and puffs on the top of her head, her eyes smiling into the camera, one graceful hand at her chin in the artificial pose favored by photographers in those days. Her forehead was exposed and there was no sign of the scar that she wore on it now.

She looked happy and life-loving, and the sight of her as she had been seventy or so years ago made Rosalie's heart ache over the inevitability of the passing years and eventual death.

More curious than ever now, interested in the Thayers as a family, Rosalie went on looking for a picture of Ezra Thayer's wife, mused over where would be the best place to find one. There were only five rooms on this floor: the drawing room, the back parlor, the big, formal dining room across the hall, the kitchen at the back of the house, the telephone cubby hole.

She eliminated four of those rooms. If there were a photograph anywhere at all, it would doubtlessly be in the back parlor, and when her mind moved to the room where she had sat with Sheriff Wellman the night before, she suddenly remembered something.

Lying on the marble-topped table had been a big, plush-covered Bible. There had been one in her own grandmother's house and she knew that such family Bibles often contained pictures of family members. She could not have said why she was so anxious to see one of Zena's mother. Perhaps the monotony that is part of every private duty case had something to do with it. There was so little diversion in her job that she was creating some. Perhaps, she admitted, she was just plain nosy.

At any rate, she went to the Bible and was pleased to find that it wasn't locked, although it had a big brass catch that held the pages together. She opened the stiff cover and at the front of the Bible there were a number of very old pictures, some of them fading.

There were those of Ezra's mother and father and one of a small child who, according to the old-fashioned script beneath it, had died at an early age. Two of Thayer men who had been lost at sea. One of Zena when she had been a child, one of her in her girlhood, one of the man she had married and who had died shortly after their son was born.

Rosalie read their histories, skimming over each. She learned that Ezra Thayer's wife, Minita, who was called "Minnie," had outlived her husband by only a few months. And that both her son and his wife had died before reaching forty but that Gloria's father had lived long enough to marry twice. One of his wives had been Gloria's mother. When he was approaching middleage, he had married a widow with a young daughter.

Philip Aldrich and his second wife, the former Juliette Merrick, had died two years ago, within months of each other. And that brought the history of the family up to the present.

So they were all dead now, all the Thayers and the Aldriches, except for Gloria and her great-grandmother, the old woman who had outlived all her descendants but one. The long-dead had left their fading pictures behind them. All of them, even those who had married into the family, had left, too, small histories of themselves.

All but Minnie. There was no picture of her and nothing at all written about her except that she had been Ezra Thayer's wife, not even a few lines about who she had been before her marriage.

Rosalie had allowed herself to become so absorbed in the past she found returning to the present a little difficult. She sat lost in thought for a few minutes before she remembered why she had come downstairs in the first place. She closed the Bible and the light sound of its pages slapping together made her start.

She still felt a little dazed as she went out of the room, down the hall and into the kitchen. The place was shadowy, the cavernous, old-fashioned cookstove and the long worktables and the big refrigerator with coils on its top looming like the oversized things seen in a ghastly nightmare.

There was something eerie about the kitchen, as though it were haunted by the ghosts of the people she had been reading about and seen pictured, as though something of them remained here in this house where they had lived and loved and mourned their dead until their own deaths.

She went quickly and quietly across the worn linoleum looking for coffee and silverware and china. She hunted for bread and made toast for herself and spread it with butter. In her search for oranges to squeeze for Mrs. Aldrich's juice, she opened the refrigerator door and found that it was almost empty. There did not seem to be much in the way of supplies anywhere, and she thought that perhaps they had simply run low and that Azie, not feeling well, had not replenished them.

Yesterday at lunch, the food had been plentiful, although there were evidences that she was beginning to see more and more clearly of scrimping and shabbiness in other quarters.

Well, she decided, she would not get on that merry-go-round of puzzlement again. She would finish her breakfast, such as it was, and squeeze the two oranges she found and get back to her patient. She would forget everything—the dead of Moontide, the odd aspects of the house—except that she was a nurse and had a job to do here.

When she reached the staircase, the glass of orange juice on a tray in one hand, Tony Chandler was coming down. He was wearing a pale blue cashmere pullover and bell-bottomed slacks and sneakers. His hair had a wind-blown look and he looked quite handsome and the fashionable sailor. He looked as though he was very much aware of it. All she felt for him was a shrinking of distaste.

He began to call out to her the moment he saw her. "Came to take Gloria out in the boat but it's too cold, she says, and that she shouldn't leave the old lady. That's a drag, isn't it? Here I am rejected, dejected, unwanted, unloved. You got a little pity to spare for a lonesome pal? Listen, they can get along without you for a couple of hours, right? Come on, get into something less starchy and I'll give you the ride of your life."

The way his eyes traveled over her made her squirm. "No chance," she told him as she started up the stairs. "I wouldn't think of it."

He put himself in her path and then began to walk down, coming closer and closer to her. She had to back away to avoid him but there was no escaping him then, either. He slid around behind her and he put both hands on her waist so that she could not go either backward or forward.

She balanced the tray gingerly so that the orange juice would not spill. There wasn't a thing she could do when he turned her around so that she was facing the front door. At that moment she saw it open and she saw the tall figure coming through it.

Immobilized by the surging of her emotions, she watched Richard Sargent stride in over the threshold.

Tony was saying, his mouth close to her ear, "Look, baby doll, forget about last night. So I struck out. But maybe I tried too hard when I got up to the plate. Give me another chance, will you? I'm not the worst guy in the world. Who knows? A few hours alone with me and you might appreciate my charms."

It was all said lightly, jeeringly, and in so low a tone that Doctor Sargent could not possibly have distinguished any of Tony's words. But even if he could not hear what was being said, Rosalie realized, he could see clearly enough what was in front of him.

Tony had taken the tray from her hand and put it on the step behind him. Then, in that moment when she could not move, he slid his arms around her. His face was close to hers. He might have just kissed her, for all Richard knew, or was on the point of doing so.

Rosalie's heart, which had leaped high at the sight of the man coming in through the door, sank heavily with dismay.

She freed herself, but it was too late by then. After hesitating for a moment while he stared at the two of them, Doctor Sargent moved forward, his black bag clutched in his hand, his face dark and tight.

Of course he thought she was dallying here, letting Gloria Aldrich's fiance make love to her while her patient lay neglected upstairs.

He passed her without a word, careful not to upset the glass of orange juice. He was walking rapidly and by the time she had freed herself from Tony's still-seeking hands and retrieved the tray, Richard was disappearing into the dusky shadows at the top of the stairs. All she could see was the rigidity of his back, the stiff angle of his head.

She hurried after him crying, "Doctor Sargent!" but he did not turn back nor answer her.

8

She was breathing hard by the time she reached the sickroom. There was only the sound of her panting as she crossed it and put the orange juice on the bedside table. She felt no longer shamed but angry that she was once more at a disadvantage where Richard was concerned. She hated the defensive role in her voice as she burst out, "Doctor Sargent, I want you to know—"

And then she stopped because as she raised her head and looked beyond him, she saw that Gloria was sitting in the chair at the other side of the room. Her hands were folded in an attitude of meekness. She looked very young and vulnerable, but every hair on her head was in place, her clothing was immaculate, her makeup was flawless. The contrast of her own rumpled appearance heightened Rosalie's flush.

She could say nothing now. It was out of the question to try to explain about Tony with Gloria within earshot. At any rate, Rosalie realized with despair, it would be useless to say anything that Richard would beileve. His face was tight and closed. The single glance that he swept over her had something contemptuous in it.

Well, let him think anything he likes, she thought as the anger burned in her cheeks. He is nothing at all to me.

When he spoke to her, it was only to ask about his patient. He examined Mrs. Aldrich and Rosalie told him about the woman's restlessness during the night. Then it was to Gloria that he turned.

He said in a gentler, more compassionate voice than Rosalie had ever heard him use before, "You mustn't put too much stock in that, there's really no cause for optimism. Her condition is unchanged."

He was sorry for Gloria, Rosalie knew, because he recognized her sorrow over her impending loss. And because he believed that while she had been sitting here keeping vigil at the bedside of the old woman she loved so deeply, another girl had snatched the opportunity to indulge in a romantic interlude with the man she was soon to marry.

He was on the point of leaving when Rosalie stopped him. "Doctor Sargent!"

When he turned, his face was without expression. "Yes, what is it?"

"What I said yesterday about leaving. I don't think we settled whether you were to notify the registry or whether I was. If you haven't already done it, please don't. I won't be going. Not right away, at any rate."

His mouth moved in a knowing, lopsided smile. "Well, sure, that figures. I guess I can understand your deciding to stay."

"I don't think you do. It wasn't my decision. And if you have a minute, I'd like to explain it to you."

She motioned him out in the hall, not wanting Gloria to be further distressed by talk of murder and police investigations. She spoke in a low voice as she told Richard how Hugo Bannister had died, had been deliberately poisoned and had not died, as had first been thought, of a heart attack.

"And I cannot leave here now. They are not—are not sure that I didn't have something to do with his murder. I do not know," she said, shaking her head as though she could clear the bewilderment out of it that way, "how in the world I ever got enmeshed in this horrible situation.

"Everything in my life up to now has been normal, ordinary." She had forgotten she was speaking to him. It was as though a dam had burst and all her puzzlement and resentment and fears went pouring out in a flood of words. "I am the least likely person in the world to get caught up in a nightmare of this sort.

"I'm just—a person. I have parents who think I'm pretty special, and I live with them. I haven't done anything in my life more exciting than go on a Mediterranean cruise once with a bunch of nurses. I date—occasionally. I bowl and go to the movies when I'm not on a case. I cringe at horror pictures and I cry at weddings. I like to read biographies and watch the news on TV. I got good nurses' training and I'm offered more jobs than I could possibly accept. I buy government bonds and I like pizza.

"Doesn't that," she cried fiercely, "sound as though I'm an average twenty-three-year old girl, maybe even that well-known girl next door? Then how did I become a candidate for a cozy little spot in the cemetery? Why? Can you tell me that? Why did you have me come to this weird place where someone is trying to kill me? It isn't enough that my life is in danger! Now I'm suspected of killing a man who was never anything but kind to me—a friend as well as a patient! Why, Doctor Sargent, did you want me here?"

"I?"

"Yes, you! Gloria said—"

As her voice soared to near-hysterical notes and then broke, he stretched his hand out to her, and then he drew it back hastily. His face, concerned for a moment, grew stiff again.

He was probably ashamed of his brief weakness and rebuilding his defenses, Rosalie thought. He was probably telling himself cynically that ordinary girls-next-door did not try to steal men who belonged to other girls.

Rosalie looked into his face and smiled brightly. It came to her suddenly that this was all very silly. All she had to do was open her mouth and tell him what it was between her and Tony Chandler—nothing. Why did she insist on pampering her pride? What good was false pride, what did it serve?

She brought to the fore a different, more meaningful sort of pride. It made her want to speak honestly and not have a member of her own profession misjudge her, to go on believing that she had acted in an unethical and wanton manner.

They were nurse and doctor. They both were aware that while she was on a case her duties were of primary importance. Personal diversions had no place in a hospital or a house where there was a dying patient.

And because she was a nurse and had her reputation as a good one to maintain, her determination stiffened and she told Doctor Sargent that he was to remain right there and listen to her explanation.

"Not justifications or excuses. I don't need to. I was an unwilling partner in that little scene you saw downstairs. Believe me, he would be the last person in the world that I'd pick. I did what I could to discourage him right from the beginning. Doctor Sargent," she said, with a tremolo of earnestness in her voice, "you must believe that I was trained in self-discipline, and with a man I do not even care for . . . if it so happened that I was madly in love with him, I would not . . ."

The words began to grow weak and then they drifted off to nothingness. She was remembering (and she was certain that he was remembering, too) that there had been a few minutes when she had been completely without self-discipline. And what she was implying (and she was sure that he realized it, too) was that she was senselessly, madly in love with him, driven mindless by her emotion so that she had abandoned all her standards and her rules for living.

There fell between them a long silence in which she could almost hear the uneven beating of her heart. Because she had to get off the subject of Tony Chandler before her confusion gave her away completely, she went back to her original reason for calling him out into the hall.

"Now you know why I've got to stay here. Even if there is someone in this house who wants me dead. Even if my life is in danger."

He looked at her thoughtfully for a moment or two and then, seeming to come to some decision, he nodded. "I'll speak to Wellman. I don't imagine he actually believes you'd take off and never be seen again if he let you leave here. I think maybe you're right, Rosalie. You've had just about enough."

He was the one who brought Tony Chandler's name between them again. "I feel sorry for that poor kid in there," and he nodded in the direction of Zena Aldrich's bedroom. "She's got a great life ahead of her with Chandler."

Rosalie watched him go down the corridor and went on standing there even after he had disappeared around the curve of the staircase.

Opening the door to honesty had made her honest with herself and she thought, "I am in love with him," and she accepted the fact of it. In spite of her strict notions of her function as a nurse, it had taken only these few encounters with Richard Sargent in the line of duty to enmesh her hopelessly with him. Hopelessly because revealing her antipathy for Tony Chandler to him had changed nothing. She was left with a one-sided love on her hands.

It was all very well to try—as she did—to tell herself that it was this house, the strange and ominous atmosphere of it and the bizarre things that had happened since her arrival that was affecting her emotions. The truth went on nagging at her. Under any circumstances, anywhere else in the world, she would have given her heart to this man who did not want it.

She went back to the sickroom. "Gloria," she said to the girl who still sat as unmoving in the chair as though she were part of it, "why don't you get out for a while and get some fresh air? You shouldn't be stuck in the house every minute of every day. I don't know why you didn't accept your fiance's invitation to go out in the boat with him. I met him downstairs," she added lamely. "He told me he had asked you."

"I just couldn't." Gloria shook her head with a jerky motion. "I have to stay here. Perhaps if she wakes up I can talk to her. Maybe I can say something that will—will make her want to go on living."

Her eyes, as she stared at her great-grandmother's nurse, were haunted. The stamp of fear was on her face. "I can't leave her alone."

"But I'll be here. And even if I have to be away from the room for a few minutes, I can get someone else to stay with her for that length of time. Azie may be well enough by then. Or Jug could surely—"

Something stronger than fear, something more like pure terror, leaped into Gloria's features. "No!" she whispered. "Oh, please, no!"

Rosalie crossed the room and bent down and took the knotted fists into her own hands. "Why are you so afraid of Azie and Jug? They are your servants, aren't they? Who hired them—you? Or have they been here for a long time, perhaps before your father died?"

Gloria spoke in such a low voice, almost a whisper, that Rosalie had to bend even closer to hear what she was saying.

"I had nothing to do with it. They've only been here a few weeks. When Grandma first became so sick. I did not want them here. We had a couple, a man and his wife. But Azie and Jug simply moved in and sent the other two away. And they—Azie and her son—just stayed on. I told them to leave but they would not. No matter what I said! They acted as though I hadn't spoken to them. They are still here, and they will go on staying until—" and her voice, rising on a light scream, broke.

"But, good Lord, that is ridiculous!" Rosalie stared down at the other girl, unbelieving. "Such a thing simply couldn't happen. You should not have allowed it. This is your home, you're in charge here. Why didn't you take some action then, right at the first when they moved in? Why didn't you call the police, for instance?"

"The police? Oh, no, I couldn't!" She was whispering again, her mouth working and trembling. "You don't understand. I couldn't do that."

Her patience beginning to fray, Rosalie said, "Well, I don't see why not! Or you could have got someone else to take care of it, couldn't you? What about Mr. Chandler? Weren't you engaged to him then? Couldn't you have told him what happened and asked his help?"

"No. You see, I haven't known Tony so very long. We met only a month ago and those two were here then. Tony and I fell in love almost at first sight and he gave me my ring a week ago. Maybe you think that's strange, our living so close to each other and not meeting. But I was away at school for years and when I was home I did not go out very much. He did; he had a large circle of friends," she said with something like pride. "There was the Army, of course, and he spent some of his summers in Europe. So it wasn't strange that we'd never happened to meet.

"It was just this past summer—at the end of it, really—that he had some trouble with his boat right off the cliffs here and he came, all wet from swimming inshore, and asked to use the telephone. It happened then between him and me," she finished simply.

Tony, Rosalie reflected, was an all-around fast worker. This gentle girl, sheltered and isolated from the world, couldn't have been anything except putty in his hands.

Sheriff Wellman had mentioned that the occupants of Moontide had lived like "hermits," but the spoiled, self-willed young man, who had obviously never been denied anything he wanted, had come across the lovely little hermit girl and swept her off her feet. He had come like a rescuing knight to free the captive princess in her tower. The love story would have had all the elements of sweet romance except for one thing. The handsome knight was a philanderer and there was not going to be any lived-happily-ever-after ending to the fairy tale. This Rosalie knew and it made her more gentle than ever when she spoke to Gloria.

"Then you could have found someone else to help you," she insisted. "You must have friends. Your stepsister, Julie. If there were two of you, it wouldn't have been so hard. Wasn't she here with you then?"

At the mention of Julie Merrick's name, Gloria's body became even stiffer and her eyes more suffering. "No," she choked, "No. I never spoke to her about Azie and Jug. She is like a guest, not a member of the household."

"I can see that," Rosalie said dryly. "She hasn't been in here once to offer to help. I haven't even seen her around today. She must be still sleeping."

"Or out with Tony."

"He was alone when I met him," Rosalie said hastily, to console her. "But I don't know why you didn't tell her about these two servants that you wanted to get rid of."

"She would have laughed at me. She's very—strong and—and self-sufficient in spite of that sweet manner she has. Once when I criticized them for something, she stood up for them, said we were lucky to have anyone at all away out here in this place. God-forsaken is what she calls this house. But still she keeps coming back every little while. Now she says she's going to stay until—until the end. I wish," she cried, her voice cracking, "that she'd go and never come back!"

"Why doesn't she? Is it the money?"

"The money?" Gloria stared up uncomprehendingly. "What do you mean?"

"Your great-grandmother will leave an estate? She must be wealthy. This big house. Some of the things downstairs look priceless. Does Julie expect a legacy perhaps?"

The other girl said shortly, "Everything will come to me. There is no one else. Julie isn't even a relative of Grandma's. No relation at all. Oh, I don't want to talk about things like that in this room! She seems to be sleeping but we can't be sure she doesn't hear us."

Rosalie, feeling rebuffed and knowing that she

had pried into things that did not concern her, left Gloria there and went to the other side of the room. For a long time there were no sounds except an occasional groan from the woman in the bed and, now and then, the noise of a motor boat far out on the ocean.

When Jug came into the room with a luncheon tray for her and Rosalie, Gloria sprang out of her chair and watched him with wide, staring eyes while he transferred the dishes from the tray to a table in the corner.

Rosalie asked, after he had left, "Is he really as feeble-minded as he seems to be or is it only something of an act? He can cook. He can drive a car. He does all right keeping this place running when his mother is incapacitated. By the way, do you think she is ill enough to need help? If you'll tell me where her room is, I could go and see."

"Don't bother. She is just old, that's all, and the work is too much for her. Exhaustion catches up with her now and then. And he's dim-witted, that's for sure."

Her mouth remained half-open after she had spoken. Her eyes had on them a sightless glaze and she did not seem to hear when Rosalie reminded her that there were sandwiches and coffee waiting.

"Drink your coffee while it's hot. You probably didn't have any breakfast, did you?"

Gloria did not answer. She ignored the food that Rosalie indicated. Since Jug had left the room, she seemed to be in an almost catatonic state. Rosalie, recognizing the symptoms of imminent breakdown—the withdrawal, the unfocused eyes, the pallor and the inability to use the voice—knew that she was facing a new crisis, another one. There seemed to be no end to them.

9

By the time mid-afternoon came, Rosalie could not stand it a moment longer. The unsuccessful attempts to get Gloria to speak, the anguish on the girl's white face, the medical smell of the sick-room, the gloom with only the paltry light from a single lamp to lighten it, the feeling of the world being closed out by the dark, heavy draperies—all combined to envelop her in a thickening cocoon of depression.

If I don't get out of here for a little while, I'll be the one that'll flip, she thought. She said to Gloria, "If you won't take a breather for at least a few minutes, then I think I will. I shan't be long. Just long enough to get a breath of fresh air. There won't be a change in your great-grandmother before I get back. I'm sure of it," and she looked critically at her patient. "If anything happens, I won't be far away. Only downstairs. I'll stay close to the house."

She had no intention of going into the grounds. "No more wandering around," Sheriff Wellman had warned her. And her own good sense precluded even a short walk in the direction of the cliffs. As for the footpath that led to the carriage house . . . The remembered fear shook her again. She went to the front door, out onto the porch and that, she decided, was exactly as far as she would go.

There was a gentle warmth in the afternoon sun. It threw a light covering of glittering sequins over the ocean that stretched beyond the cliffs. A slight, salt-filled breeze riffled the skirt of her uniform and here, with the stark beauty of the blue sky and blue water and golden sunlight everywhere within her vision, the horrors of death and danger seemed far away and unrealistic.

The porch was wide and it stretched around three sides of the house. On the side facing the driveway, articles of summer furniture, out of use but not yet put away, were pushed against the wall of the house. Basket chairs had peeling paint and old-fashioned rockers creaked as they were suddenly moved by the wind. The sound was eerie as it broke the silence.

Rosalie's mood of tranquility was broken, too, and her thoughts went racing back to the past again. She wondered who had occupied the chairs, who had sat here in summers past listening to the pounding of the surf and the complaining cry of a gull as it swooped down over the water. Was this as far as Zena Aldrich, that hermitlike figure never seen by her fellow townspeople, ever ventured? Were her son and his wife, and then Gloria's father and either of his two wives, addicted to porch-sitting?

Had either of the two young ladies of the house, Gloria or Julie, sat here with young men and watched the sunset staining the horizon? Held hands in the twilight? Kissed in the darkness? Not Gloria, surely, the captive princess who had waited for her shoddy young knight. Julie, possibly. There was more to her than appeared on the surface.

She might be recklessly in love with Tony Chandler now but Rosalie was certain that he was only one in a long line of men. She did not know why she was so sure of that. She simply was.

Thinking about Julie brought back a feeling of uneasiness. She wondered again why the girl had not put in an appearance all day. It was not, of course, any of her business. What she was concerned about was that Julie was sneaking out to meet Tony and that Gloria would find out about it. Rosalie did not want another patient on her hands. Gloria was close to the breaking point now.

When she felt that she had remained there long enough and knew that Gloria might be growing nervous over her absence, Rosalie started back toward the front door. And then halted uncertainly because she heard the sound of a motor coming up the lane. It was faint at first and then grew louder, as did the noise of tires crunching on the clam shells.

The car drew up to the foot of the steps. A woman got out of it and slammed its door purposefully. She came striding, with no hesitation, up to where Rosalie was standing, stopped close to her and shifted her handbag from one arm to the other.

Rosalie had never seen the woman before but she was evidently recognized because a tight mouth opened, sharp eyes raced over her uniform and a voice that sounded carefully modulated said, "You're Miss Dexter."

It was not a question but a statement and one which defied contradiction. The long chin was held up firmly. The green-flecked eyes stared steadily. The woman was not attractive. Her mouth was too thin and too straight, and her skin appeared to be stretched too tightly over sharp bones. But her makeup was flawless and her clothing was striking. She wore a beautifully cut suit of pale green wool, alligator shoes and a hat that seemed to have been fashioned from a single feather of some rare bird. At her throat there was a pin that looked costly. Matching diamonds winked in her ear lobes.

Everything about her was spoiled by her disagreeable manner and the imperiousness with which she held herself while she waited impatiently for Rosalie to speak.

"Yes, I'm her—she, I mean."

"Who else? Who else indeed?" The woman ducked her head, took a cigarette from her handbag, lit it with a gold lighter and then peered at Rosalie through the smoke. "Miss Dexter, the sweet, kind, helpful, self-seeking Miss Dexter!"

Her gaze went traveling again. "Yes, I guess you could get around Uncle Hugo easily enough. I can see why now. You're young, you're pretty in a plebeian sort of way," she said grudgingly. "And he wouldn't be the first middleaged fool to fall for his nurse."

"I do not know," Rosalie said, growing hot and flushed with anger, "what in the world you're talking about. Just who are you, anyway?"

"Louise Bannister Gregory. Do call me Mrs. Gregory." Her smile was merely a mocking loosening of her lips and a brief showing of her small, white teeth. "I'm his niece. Hugo's. The man you worked for and whom you managed to wind around your little finger. Worked for—and on. Made a blithering fool of for your own purposes."

Rosalie shook her head. "I haven't the slightest idea what this is all about. I think you'd better tell me. Do you want to come inside?" She waved toward the door. "Or we can stay out here. Either way, let's get it settled."

She took a step toward one of the basket chairs, but Louise Gregory stopped her.

"Don't bother. I can say all I have to say in a few short words. I want Hugo's book back."

"You—what?"

"I assume your hearing is normal. So you must have heard what I said. I speak distinctly enough, I think."

"Heard, yes. Understood, no."

The unpleasant smile came and went again. "It's simple enough to understand. Just what I said, Miss Dexter. I expect you to return Uncle Hugo's manuscript to me. My brother and I are the legal heirs. It says so quite plainly in the will. Everything Hugo owned was left to us. Surely you've been able to follow me this far."

Her features seemed to draw together in an expression of shrewdness. "What we think, Frank and I, is that Hugo wanted to leave you something but that you both knew we could break the will if there was anything of great value that came your way. Undue influence, they call it. A nurse doesn't have much chance when it's a terminal case and she only came on the scene a few weeks before death occurred.

"My brother," she cried triumphantly, "is a lawyer. And he said—Frank said—that any recent will of Hugo's could have been broken without too much trouble. And so he—Hugo, that is—passed that book on to you for safekeeping because, according to what he wrote me in one letter, it was 'dynamite.' Then, when you got your hands on it, you couldn't bear to give it back. So you hurried him on his way!"

Rosalie could barely bring her voice out of a throat that had constricted with horror. "That's monstrous! How can you stand there and say a thing like that to my face? It's a dreadful lie. I was not even there when he died—when he was killed. It was my day off."

"Oh, nurses!" Louise Gregory's laugh was like a drawn-out sneer. "As though there wouldn't have been some way you could have given him a poison with delayed effects! That's probably exactly what happened."

Rosalie could not believe what she was hearing. The ghastliness of the accusation had snatched away her ability to think clearly, to speak coherently. She said the first thing that came into her mind.

"Does Sheriff Wellman believe that?" and then she realized, appalled, how guilty she sounded with her concern about whether or not she appeared guilty in the eyes of the law. She burst out, "None of it is true, of course! I never even saw the book except when he was writing it. He kept it locked away when he wasn't working on it."

Mrs. Gregory shrugged. "I have no real interest in what the authorities do or do not believe. There's going to be an inquest in a day or two. I imagine you'll be called as a witness and you can tell your little tale of innocence then. All I'm interested in is getting back what belongs to Frank and me."

Rosalie said slowly, as calmness returned to her, "Mr. Bannister must have been fairly rich. He lived in that beautiful house with all those wonderful furnishings. He did not work except to write and he told me that he had been doing that, full time, for several years. So there must have been quite a bit of money. The inheritance, which you and your brother are to share, should be substantial. Why then," she asked with genuine curiosity, "are you so worried about this one little detail of the estate?"

"Because it belongs to us." She spoke petulantly and her face had become waspish. "Because we want everything that's coming to us. Hugo had sent a copy of the manuscript, as much as he had done, to a publisher who was all ready to make him an advance. We want that. It belongs to us now. And whatever else there is coming when the book is published."

And so, Rosalie thought, it is all out in the open; the purpose of the visit was no longer hidden.

Here was greed. She could see it in the green-flecked eyes that were too close to the frail nose and in the pursing mouth. Just how much money could have been realized on a book written by a man of Hugo Bannister's sedentary habits she could not accurately guess. Not very much, she imagined. But whatever it was, Louise Gregory wanted it, every last cent.

"I don't know anything about the book," she

told the woman again. "I never even found out what it was about. And I certainly can't return it if I haven't got it, now can I?"

"We will see." Defeat brought mottled color into Louise Gregory's cheeks. "You must have it. Where else could it be? I thought perhaps that it was Benjamin, the manservant—you know? He gets something, a very generous legacy, but I figured he might have thought it wasn't enough. I don't think it was Benjamin, though. He's poorly educated and we questioned him vigorously, Frank and I. He convinced us he knows nothing about the book. So that leaves only you, doesn't it?"

Poor Benjamin Choate! A picture of the quiet, elderly man who had served Hugo Bannister long and faithfully rose in Rosalie's mind. White-haired, soft-spoken, always on hand when she needed him, he had come to seem like a friend to her while she had been in the big house that looked out over the water on Harbor View Drive.

Poor Benjamin! They must have given him an extremely bad time and she could imagine that: the sharp, querulous voices, the pouncing on any contradiction of terms, the pointed questions until the poor old man had probably been confused to the point of tears. They would have been merciless with him because he had been remembered in their uncle's will and thus had taken from them something they felt was rightfully theirs.

She remained calm under Mrs. Gregory's probing eyes and finally the woman lifted her shoulders, shifting her handbag again and made a little leave-taking motion.

"If you persist in refusing, then there is nothing

I can do for you. I shall insist that the law take its course. We shall remain here, Frank and I, until that is settled. My husband will have to get along without me for a few more days while I stay here and see that justice is done."

10

SHE TOSSED her cigarette over the porch railing, turned on her heel and went down the steps to where the car was waiting. It wasn't the big black one that Benjamin Choate had used for doing Mr. Bannister's errands but the smaller one that had stood in the garage behind the house. Her brother, Rosalie guessed, had claimed the other one for his own, no doubt; between them they would have snatched at everything they could lay their hands on.

A mail truck came along while Mrs. Gregory was making the turn in the driveway. She went sweeping past it, her fender missing its hood by only inches. Rosalie stood waiting until the driver of the truck, looking a little white-faced, climbed down from it and came over to her shaking his head.

"Some women drivers!" He breathed gustily. "You Rosalie Dexter?" He had a package under his arm. When she nodded, he pushed it at her and then handed her a pencil and a slip of paper. "Want to sign for it, please?"

While she wrote her name, she said, "I can't imagine who would be sending me anything," but he was not interested, took back his pencil and the receipt and went back to his truck. She watched him go. He seemed like a link with the outside world, the place where she felt comfortable, and where a parcel post package was an everyday occurrence.

When she had been on cases that had drawn out longer than she had expected them to, her mother had sometimes sent her requested articles. But she had not called home since her arrival, and even if she had asked to have anything sent, there would not have been time for it to be delivered. She could scarcely believe that she had been here for such a short time. It seemed like a lifetime with all sorts of strange and horrible and unexplainable things crowded into it.

The reason why she had not called home was because she had a mother with some sort of sixth sense for detecting unhappiness or agitation, even through a telephone wire, no matter how much blandness or cheeriness Rosalie tried to put into her voice. Mom would have said, after the first few words her daughter spoke, "You get home here immediately, you hear me? Or do you want me to drive right up there and make you leave?"

She would have done it, too. Mom still wasn't convinced that nursing was the right profession for a carefully-reared young lady. In a day or two, if Rosalie hadn't called her by then, she could expect to hear her mother's anxious voice on the telephone.

But I will doubtlessly be gone by then, she told herself, remembering suddenly the dying woman upstairs. Remembering, too, that she had been away from the sickroom much too long. By this time, Gloria might be out of her mind—

literally—with worry. Rosalie went speeding up the stairs.

Her heart plunged when she looked down at her patient. Even during her short absence, there had been a change in Mrs. Aldrich's condition. It had not been a change for the better. The mouth was more cyanotic. The breathing was more labored. When Rosalie put her fingers on the woman's wrist, she could scarcely feel a pulse.

Gloria had been watching her with widened, fearful eyes. "I think," Rosalie said as quietly as she could in order not to alarm her more, "that you had better go and call Doctor Sargent. In cases like this, there are apt to be setbacks. I don't want to take full responsibility. It won't hurt to have the doctor here."

The girl fled from the room and Rosalie, knowing that she was going to have a long evening and a longer night ahead of her, drew a chair closer to the bedside. On its seat, where she had dropped them were her sweater and the package. She picked them up and carried them into the adjoining bedroom. Because Richard was coming, she could not resist glancing into the mirror over the dressing table. It was a small vanity and she was a little ashamed of it because at a time like this she should be thinking of him only as her patient's doctor.

She left the door open between the two rooms and put her sweater in the drawer of a dresser and the package on top of it. In her haste, she had not yet glanced at the return address on it and now she did, read the careful printing with a little start of surprise.

"From—Benjamin Choate," it said. "297 Harbor View Drive." The address was a familiar one. It was the one where she had lived while she was taking care of Hugo Bannister.

How had Benjamin known where she was? The answer came easily. He had probably called the registry. The next question was more of a poser. Why should he be sending her something in a square, well-wrapped package?

She went in to look at Mrs. Aldrich again, saw that there was nothing she could do for her at the moment and then went in search of her surgical scissors. The twine on the package was securely knotted and she cut it away, removed the brown wrapping paper and found a square white box beneath it.

Clipped to it was a small bit of notepaper on which was written, "It seemed best that you should have this. Yrs. truly, Benj. Choate."

Best? Best for what? Rosalie asked herself. Her puzzlement deepened and she put the note aside and went back to the box. She saw that a sticker had been pasted directly in the middle of the cover and on the sticker were typed the words, SECRETS OF AN OLD TOWN, BY HUGO BANNISTER.

Her questions were answered. Before she lifted the cover from the box, Rosalie knew that she would find inside the manuscript of Hugo Bannister's book. The title was repeated on the first sheet of paper. The one under that was the dedication page.

It read, "To the memory of my old friend, Philip Cromwell Aldrich, whose idea this was originally and whose sharing of many of the 'secrets' made this book possible."

It was a thick manuscript. more than three hundred pages double-spaced, and Rosalie knew that it would take her hours and hours to read it.

She had no time for that now. She should not be delaying here and she would most certainly be needed in the room next door when Gloria returned. Mrs. Aldrich's death undoubtedly would be only a matter of hours. It would be the girl who would need attention, who could quickly slide, if Rosalie had read the symptoms correctly, into a whirlwind of hysteria.

As soon as she comes back, Rosalie temporized. I can just take a peek at this with one eye on the other room and keep my ears open.

The temptation was too strong. And her attention had been caught by something on a typewritten page of the first chapter. Hugo Bannister had set forth on it the story of a long-ago scandal that had happened here in Stoneport.

It was the account of a young wife who had grown tired of her middle-aged husband and fallen in love with a youth who had come in one of the sailing ships to what had been then a lively port. The husband had found the two lovers together and had stabbed them both to death with the knife he used for slashing fish. Then he had hung their bodies from his roof tree so that all the women in the village might be taught a lesson. And he was never seen again, had sailed away in his boat in the dead of night leaving his grisly specimens behind him.

It was a horrible story. Rosalie, shuddering, remembered that she had passed that house, the small, gray-shingled Howard house, hundreds of times in her life without being aware of its tragic history.

She was stunned to discover this about Hugo Bannister, that he had intended to expose the heinous secret of one of his neighbors' family. He had seemed such a compassionate, well-intentioned man. This was sheer cruelty. Even though the story he had written about was long in the past, the figures in the horrifying drama long since dead. He had dug deep into the mire of an old scandal, an old crime that had taken place in the village that had always been his home. If this was any example of what the rest of the book contained, the publication of it would have caused agonizing embarrassment to perhaps a number of people.

Now, at last, she was willing to accept the fact of his murder. Here in this book was undoubtedly the answer to the question about why he had been killed. He had written to his niece about "threats," about people who did not want the book published. Now Rosalie could understand.

But why, she wondered, had not Benjamin Choate destroyed the manuscript the moment he found it? Why, of all people in the world, had he sent it to her?

Remembering Benjamin as she had known him, she realized why. Probably, since from his early youth, he had been as he was now—at home only within the confines of his narrow little world, used to being given orders and obeying them, such things as his initiative and self-reliance never developed.

Doubtlessly he had felt lost and cast adrift with Hugo Bannister's death, and with no one to tell him what to do with the manuscript his master had guarded so carefully, he had felt impelled to shift the responsibility for it to someone else. Perhaps he had been aware, in some manner, that it contained the key to the murder of the man he had depended on, loved and served for so many years.

Or perhaps there was something more to it. Hugo Bannister might have said to him, "If anything happens to me, I want you to see that Miss Dexter gets my book. I want her to have something." Among the spite and malice of Louise Gregory's accusations, there might have been this grain of truth—that her uncle had wanted to leave his nurse a legacy of some sort. It could easily have been that way.

She lifted the pages and looked at them without really reading anything until she came to the chapter, fifty or so pages into the book, that was headed: THE THAYERS, THE ALDRICHES AND THE MALEKALA.

Malekala? Rosalie wrinked her forehead. She had never seen in print or heard spoken that word in her entire life. She could not bear to put away the manuscript now. Just another moment or two, she told herself, knowing that she had to find out what it was that Hugo had written about the people in this house. Her eyes swept from one side of the chapter's first page to the other.

There was a description of the house and

grounds. "This great house, 'Moontide,' that sits overlooking the ocean from its cliff, hides the greatest, most fantastic secret of all. It was built by Ezra Thayer, richest and most prominent of so many sea captains in the village in those days. What sort of home was it? Let us consider the man first and decide whether or not he stamped it with his own personality.

"He was a cold formidable man, much feared by the members of his crew who hated him for his cruelty and his greed. It is difficult for us, when we consider the sin he committed, to accept the fact that he fell in love with a passion that surprised those who knew only his harsh and hard-hearted character. The fires must have burned savagely (and how appropriate that word is!) in his breast, for the woman who stirred his unbridled lust was the daughter of the Malekala, queen of the Saluans. Salua was inhabited by a tribe of uncivilized natives, a gem of beauty in the Pacific, at which Ezra Thayer's ship was forced to stop in order to repair a disabled sail.

"The captain met and fell in love with Minita, daughter of the queen—Malekala, in their native language, and fell prey to the beasts of desire that raged within him. According to the stories by his crew members, he kidnaped the queen's daughter in the dark of night and carried her back to this New England shore where he married her and built for her this great house, Moontide.

"The Saluan tribe had as its chief idol a moon goddess—women, it seemed, were dominant in their civilization. They were said to have many strange customs connected with the worship of their moon goddess and perhaps, in an effort to please his young bride, Captain Thayer named his house as he did."

Absorbed, Rosalie could hear her breath being drawn in, then being released, then drawn in again in regular rhythm. Then she heard something else. There came, so loud that it seemed to shatter her eardrums, a long, wailing scream. It sent her leaping up from the bed where she had sat and read the strange and disturbing manuscript.

11

WAVE AFTER WAVE, note climbing after note, the shrill screaming went on while Rosalie raced across the room, stumbled at the threshold, clung to the door jamb to regain her balance. The shrieking seemed to fill every corner of the room behind her and the one in front of her.

Gloria stood in that one, at the foot of the bed, screeching like a wild thing. Her head was thrown back and her throat was arched. Her voice gurgled and died. She drew a long breath that shuddered through her body and another scream began and stopped abruptly because Rosalie rushed across the space that had separated them. She seized the girl's shoulders and shook them roughly.

"Stop it! Stop it right this minute."

The shuddering grew more violent. Gloria's eyes were glassy and unmoving. When she opened her mouth to shriek again, Rosalie raised her hand and sent a sharp slap against the other girl's cheek. The echo of the sound of the impact seemed to hang on the air for a moment. Gloria stood as though stunned and then life came back into her eyes and the rigidity drained out of her body.

She began to cry in a childish fashion, her sobs coming in spurts. A great flood of tears poured from her eyes and she let them roll down her cheeks, made no attempt to wipe them away.

When she lifted her hand, it was to touch the spot on her face where Rosalie had struck her.

She whimpered accusingly, "You hit me! And you—you hurt me."

"There was nothing else to do. Don't you realize what a racket you were making? Gloria, you've got to get a grip on yourself. What brought this all on anyway?"

She was almost certain where she would find the answer and she turned to look at the woman in the bed. Zena Aldrich had shifted her position. She lay on her back. Her jaw had dropped and her eyes had fallen back in her head.

At first, Rosalie thought that life had left the old body. But when she went to her patient's side and felt for a heartbeat, she detected a weak and uneven flutter.

"She's dead!" Gloria sobbed. "Grandma is gone, isn't she?"

"No, she is not. Not yet."

Rosalie straightened up and went back to where the girl stood hugging herself in an attitude of anguish, her face tear-drenched, her eyes still swimming. It would be no kindness to Gloria to lie to her now, Rosalie knew. The blow, when she had believed her great-grandmother to be dead, had been a bad one. Perhaps the one facing her would be easier to bear.

"She's still alive but she won't be for long. It's only a matter of time. Listen, dear, you knew this was coming. You've got to keep control of yourself."

Rosalie took a paper handkerchief from a box by the bedside and took it to Gloria. She waited until she had mopped her face. Then she said. "I know you love her. And I know you don't want the last thing she hears to be your grief. You've got to be strong. I wish there were something I could do for her but there isn't. You called the doctor?"

Gloria nodded mutely. "He said he'd be right over."

"Then all we can do is wait. Why don't you go into the other room and lie down? When the doctor comes, he'll give you something to make all this easier for you."

"I will not let him give me anything! I will not take any medicine!" The wispy voice was no more than a whisper. "I must have—I must keep my wits about me. Don't leave me!" she begged, plucking at Rosalie's sleeve. "Please, please stay with me!"

Rosalie put a comforting hand on the slender shoulder. She could feel the shivering of the flesh under her fingers. Gloria's eyes had become like glass marbles again and her mouth kept working, even after she had stopped speaking. Collapse, it seemed certain, was not far away. There might come at any moment another outburst like the one that had sent Rosalie rushing to the girl's side.

"Look, if you'll just go in and lie down on the bed for a little while, we can leave the door open between the two rooms. That would be the same as my being with you, wouldn't it?" Rosalie coaxed, and when Gloria seemed about to weaken, she was about to press her advantage. Then her lips came together suddenly, locking inside what she had been about to say.

For she had remembered something. Mentioning the bed must have brought into her mind the realization that she had been sitting on it reading the manuscript of Hugo Bannister's book. The pages of the manuscript were still there where she had dropped them when she had heard Gloria screaming.

She had read enough of what Hugo Bannister had written to realize that it was not something to be left lying carelessly around. Especially now, with Gloria in her agitated state, it would be unwise for her to have thrust at her the secrets and scandals of people she knew and, it seemed certain, of her own family.

Eventually, something would have to be done about the manuscript. The motive for Mr. Bannister's murder, Rosalie was almost certain, had something to do with the book he had written. She would have to turn it over to the police at the first possible moment. Until she was able to do that, the responsibility for keeping it safe fell upon her.

She said, "I left something on the bed. I'll clear it away and then you can lie down there. Gloria, I want you to do this. No more nonsense now!" She spoke as though to a child, and like a child, Gloria wept and protested and tried to cling to Rosalie, but finally, under a stronger will, succumbed to authority.

"Wait here," Rosalie told her. "I'll fix the bed and be back in a minute."

She went into the bedroom next door and gathered up the typewritten sheets and put them in order back in their box. She tried to figure out the best place to hide it and decided on her suitcase which had a lock on it and a key which she kept in her handbag. She put into the suitcase the box and the wrapping paper and the note Benjamin Choate had sent her. Then she locked the suitcase and pushed it far back in the closet behind the hangers that held her clothing.

There was a quilt on the shelf of the closet and she took that down and spread it over the bed. Then she went back to Gloria and turned her around and pushed her gently into the other bedroom.

"Like it or not," she said firmly, "here is where you stay for a while. You are going to have a little rest. When the doctor comes or if there is any change in your great-grandmother's condition, I will call you. Until then, I don't want to hear a peep out of you."

In an abrupt change of attitude, Gloria seemed to have suddenly become docile. She allowed Rosalie to lead her to the bed, to remove her shoes, to spread the quilt over her. She did not even make any objections when Rosalie said, "I really think the door should be shut, though. If it's open, you'll be straining your ears to find out if there's anything going on in the other room. It would be better if you could close everything out of your mind completely and just relax.

There did not seem to be any fight left in Gloria. She nodded agreement in an exhausted manner. Rosalie tiptoed out, pulled the door softly behind her and marveled at how easy the small victory had been. She felt relieved for she knew that ahead of her lay the ordeal of the vigil that could have only one ending.

She drew up a chair and sat down beside the woman who would be her patient for only a little while longer. Life flickered faintly in the frail old body now. What was amazing was that the lowering flame had not gone out before this. Zena Aldrich was leaving the world reluctantly but quietly; her almost-imperceptible breathing went on for the next hour.

Anxious for the doctor's arrival, Rosalie got up once and went to pull back the draperies at the window that overlooked the front of the house. The weather had turned disagreeable. There were thick, unbroken clouds hiding the sky, and the surf was lashing against the rocks to make a sound like rolling thunder.

Even through the window, Rosalie could feel the raw chill of a rising wind. The prospect of the coming night sent an icy uneasiness rushing through every part of her body. Death in itself did not frighten her. But if the death watch went on and on through the dark hours, she would have to remain in this gloom-filled, danger-laden place which seemed to be haunted by the ghosts of old sorrows, old tragedies, old secrets.

She thought again of Hugo Bannister's book, remembered a certain phrase in the chapter about the Thayers and the Aldriches. "The most fantastic secret of all." It undoubtedly meant what had happened to the unhappy little bride of an iron-willed sea captain, the native Saluan girl who had been stolen from her island home and her family and brought to live in a strange land with a man she did not even know.

Rosalie longed to go and get the manuscript and read the rest of the story but she dismissed the yearning as out of the question. Gloria, she hoped, was asleep in the other room. She could not leave her patient at any rate. She must remain here and wait for Richard.

And where was he? Why hadn't he rushed to the side of the dying old woman when Gloria had called him?

He came finally, apologizing for the delay. He had run into a traffic accident shortly after he had left his office. The driver of one of the cars had been badly injured and Richard had had to rush him to the hospital.

"I am truly sorry," the doctor said. "I got here as soon as I possibly could. You're all alone? Where is Miss Aldrich?"

Rosalie motioned in the direction of the next room. "I practically forced her to get some rest."

He nodded. "She'll need it, poor kid," and he went to the bed, checked the chart and then checked Mrs. Aldrich's pulse and listened to her heart. When he straightened up, his eyes met Rosalie's and they exchanged knowledgeable glances.

This was the moment that moved and sobered men and women in the medical profession. This was the acknowledgment of defeat by the common enemy—Death. It could not be helped, their eyes consoled each other. There was nothing either of them could do. In this case, the one they were losing had lived her ninety-odd years, well over her allotted span on earth. It was battling uselessly for young ones, they both knew, that was heart-breaking: the baby who never had a chance at life; the young people dead in senseless accidents; the youthful mother or father taken from their children.

Doctor Sargent turned away and reached for his bag. All that remained now was the injection that would not stave off demise but only prolong life long enough for those who wished to be there at the end to say goodbye.

"Are there any others?" he asked with a glance at the closed door on the other side of the room. "If so, you can call them together."

"All the family she had was Gloria. Unless you can count Julie Merrick who is her grandson's step-daughter. No relation at all to Mrs. Aldrich. I haven't seen her at all today. I don't think—I'm almost sure she wouldn't care to be here."

As soon as the injection had been given, Rosalie went to rouse Gloria but it wasn't necessary. The girl wasn't asleep. She was merely lying there staring at the ceiling, her slender body stiff and motionless under the quilt. When Rosalie spoke to her, she pulled herself up into a sitting position and cried shrilly, "Is it all over?"

"No, not yet. But it will be soon. We thought you'd like to come in and say goodbye to her."

Zena Aldrich died peacefully. With scarcely more than a loud sigh, she seemed to sink even further into the bed. A hush fell over the room and in that vacuum of stillness there was not even the sound of breathing.

Doctor Sargent put the disc of his stethoscope

on the motionless chest. He straightened up again and said, "I pronounce this woman dead."

Gloria, who had been standing at the foot of the bed, swayed and would have fallen if Rosalie had not caught her. She stood there moaning and sighing in measured rhythm until the doctor turned and said, "I had better give her something."

Then she cried, "No! No!" and backed away from him. "Please, please, do not touch me! Just let me alone. I don't want anything. I don't want—anybody. I just want to be by myself."

She began to move sideways across the room and when she reached the door that led to the other bedroom, she sidled through it and slammed it shut behind her. The click of its lock sounded loud in the stillness.

Rosalie looked uncertainly at the doctor. "Do you think we should leave her alone?"

"It's hard to tell. Sometimes they come through with flying colors once they've accepted the inevitable. It's tough luck but I have to get back to the hospital. That man who got smashed up in his car may have to have surgery, if he's up to it. They're doing the tests now.

"I don't," he said, frowning at her, "like to leave you alone here, just in case she comes apart when the shock wears off. Why don't you see if you can locate that step-sister you spoke about, so you'll have help if you need it."

Rosalie said doubtfully, "Well, I can try. I don't like to hold you up. Somebody else needs you more than I do."

"I'll wait," he said, "until you get back."

She hurried off in search of Julie. She went swiftly down the second-floor hall, not able to see where she was going because no one, on this dark late afternoon, had turned on any lights along this dusky stretch.

The light switch was at the other end of the corridor. To reach it, she had to go past the worn spot on the rug and closed doors on either side of her. They gave her a feeling of malaise, although she was certain that no one could be lurking behind them. It was the presence of death in the house, the darkness, her own cowardice that she was willing to acknowledge, that spread the icy fingers of fear along her nerves.

She breathed a deep sigh of relief when her fingers pressed the button of the light switch and the low-watt bulb bloomed into a dull glow.

It was not much but it was better than nothing. It showed her the way when she went back down the corridor, opening door after door. It threw a little lightening on the shadows inside them. She was able to see that all of them were empty and that only one of them looked as though anyone had occupied it recently.

That one was furnished in various shades of pink that looked purple in the feeble light. Its dressing table held a collection of perfume bottles and makeup jars. There was something in the pervasive scent that suggested Julie. But Julie was not in her room and when Rosalie went downstairs, looked into the drawing room and the back parlor and the dining room and the empty kitchen, her searching remained futile.

The whole house seemed to be wrapped in an

unearthly stillness. Rosalie stopped when she reached the bottom of the staircase again because she thought she heard the sound of a car in the lane. She stood waiting, but the sound came no further. Not Julie, Rosalie decided. It was someone who had taken the narrow path to Moontide by mistake, had turned around on discovering the mistake and gone back the way he had come from.

Not Julie who, Rosalie suspected, had seen Tony going off alone and run after him and begged him to take her with him. Undoubtedly they had kept a rendezvous on his boat and were probably, at this very moment, sipping cocktails in the Yacht Club bar after spending the afternoon together. It was the only explanation for the absence of the both of them.

Rosalie went back to report her lack of success to Richard.

"I've looked everywhere I could think of. She must have left the house and not returned yet. Well, it will be all right. I can handle anything that comes up and I can stay as long as necessary. It's part of the job."

He smiled at her and her heart leaped at the shine of approval in his eyes. "You're a good nurse, Rosalie. Don't think I don't realize that." He stopped speaking and his eyes looked deep into hers. "I wish we had gotten off to a better start. You think we could go back to the beginning and start all over again?"

In another minute, she knew, she would be a helpless mess. All she needed was a couple of kind words and she was sunk. That other time . . .

The memory of that other time rose vividly in her mind and she summoned up all her good sense. She was not going to let herself be inveigled into acting like such a complete idiot again.

She stretched her mouth into a false, cold smile and she forced lightness into her voice.

"Sure, why not?" she chirped. "We'll probably be running into each other from time to time. So you may be sure, Doctor Sargent—oh, you can bank on it, Doctor—that I shall be quite as deferential, as admiring as all the other nurses you come in contact with. How will that be?"

His face tightened and he sighed. "That again? All right, Rosalie, little thorny Rose. We'll be as professional as all get out, if you say so. It could have been great, but never mind."

He picked up his bag, started for the door and then stopped. "I think I'd better take another look at Miss Aldrich, just to make sure you won't get embroiled in a crisis here. Then I'll be on my way."

She walked with him to the door of the adjoining bedroom. It was locked and Gloria did not respond to their knocking. Rosalie, alarmed, ran out into the hall and to the door of the bedroom there. It opened easily under her hand and she went into the room with Richard following her.

So she was the one who saw first the empty bed.

12

There was no one in the room. Rosalie searched it thoroughly, even opening the closet door and pushing aside the clothing on its hangers. When Doctor Sargent asked, "What in the world?" she answered, "Because I thought she might have gone in there and fainted. But evidently not."

He said, "She's probably just gone to get a drink of water. Or something stronger. Maybe that's what she decided she needed right now."

"But I didn't see her!" Rosalie protested. It was wearing off, that first shock of not finding Gloria in her room, and a thick cloud of apprehension was taking its place. Her voice shook a little. "I was downstairs and I looked in the kitchen and the other rooms. Why didn't I see her or meet her somewhere along the line? Unless . . ."

And then she broke off because there was in her throat a thick column of fear.

"Unless what?"

"Unless it was arranged that I wouldn't see her." Rosalie lifted a hand and pushed a lock of hair off a forehead that had grown damp. "This is a big house, you know. And sort of—sort of complicated. There seem to be passageways leading to the ells and additions. This is the main part but I don't know how many rooms there are that I haven't seen yet.

"The staircase that comes up from the front hall can't be the only one in this place. There has to be a back one. So if Gloria were—were taken from this room down the other end of the corridor, it could be done without you or I knowing anything about it."

Richard crossed the space that separated them and took hold of her shoulder and shook it lightly. "Rosalie, what kind of crazy chatter is this? You sound like somebody in a bad movie. What are you talking about—kidnaping? You private duty nurses are alone too much, have too much time to dream up weird ideas. Honey, can you hear what you're saying? That you're in the middle of some sort of lunatic nightmare."

She looked straight into his face. "Yes," she said more evenly. "That is it. That's the way it is. Twice—although you evidently thought I was dreaming then, too—somebody tried to kill me. And Gloria was terrified for her safety. She was broken up about her great-grandmother's terminal illness, sure. But she wouldn't have been so—so hysterical if there weren't something she was more frightened of.

"Mrs. Aldrich's dying was minor, I think, compared to what was really troubling her. Today, all day today, she was almost paralyzed by fear. I think she knew that someone meant to harm her. She refused to take any medication. She had to keep her wits about her, she said. Why should the impending death of an old, old lady affect her like that? Sorrow, yes, that was to be expected. But not terror."

"Who?" Doctor Sargent asked bluntly. "Who

do you think she was afraid of, was supposed to mean her harm?"

Rosalie moved her head back and forth in a helpless gesture. "I don't know. That's just it. Although, to be honest, I do have my suspicions. She was scared to death of the servants, Azie and Jug. I saw the way she looked and acted when the man came into the room today. This wasn't something that just came on her recently. She wanted to get rid of them but she was too afraid of them to send them away."

She told Richard the story that Gloria had told her, how the two servants had forced their way into the household.

"But I don't think the real danger was from them. Why should an old woman who's half blind and a dim-witted man want to kill someone they never saw until a few weeks ago? Unless they were persuaded to do it by someone else? I can think of only one reason—money. Maybe they were promised an enormous sum—more money than they had ever seen before or ever will see again."

It was all pouring out now, all the vague conjectures and suspicions that had not, until now, crystallized to form a solid theory. Her voice became louder and firmer.

"Now that Mrs. Aldrich is dead, Gloria will inherit the estate. She told me that. Everything will come to her. But if she dies, there is only one person who would have any claim at all on the Aldrich fortune. Gloria has only one relative left in the world."

Richard's laugh was low and uneasy. "Oh, come

on! You don't actually mean that you think there was a plot against that young lady's life? Hired killers, all that? A couple of people brought in to murder her after her great-grandmother died? All right, say it. Let's have the whole bit. Who is it who'd benefit from Gloria's death? What's the name of the person who would get the house and the fortune and everything she inherited from Mrs. Aldrich?"

He stood waiting and she said it. She spoke the name in such a low and unwilling voice that he did not hear it the first time and she had to repeat it.

"Julie Merrick."

When he started to speak, she raised a hand and silenced him. "It isn't only the money. Julie's in love with Tony Chandler."

He said drily, "That guy sure gets around."

"No, but listen. Don't you see how everything adds up? I heard Julie threaten Gloria. She said she was going to get Tony no matter what she had to do. And Julie's been out of sight all day long. I thought maybe she had sneaked out with Tony, but now I don't know. Perhaps she was just waiting, hiding some place, until Mrs. Aldrich died.

"Because don't you see? It wouldn't have done her any good at all if Gloria had predeceased her great-grandmother. There was no relationship between Mrs. Aldrich and Julie. And there's not even a blood tie between her and Gloria. But maybe she's found out that it's enough for her to inherit what Gloria would have had. And I think Gloria knew all this, too, and that's why she was so terrified of Azie and Jug—because she suspected that Julie brought them here for just that purpose."

"And you," he asked, "where do you come into all this?"

She could feel the sourness on her lips when she smiled at him.

"You still don't believe me, do you, Doctor? You still think I've got an overactive imagination and that everything that happened to me—the linen closet, the near-suffocation in the carriage house—are just things I dreamed up to amuse myself and help pass the time. You do, don't you?"

"Just let me ask you this. What's your part in what you've told me? If it's true, what you believe about Miss Aldrich and her step-sister, why should anyone be out to kill you?"

They had been standing close together and now he moved even nearer, so near that she could smell the disinfectant on his hands and the faint aroma of shaving lotion from his cheeks. He seemed unaware that she was growing more flushed and agitated. And that she was keeping her eyes turned away for fear that what she felt for him would show in them.

"Well, Rosalie, what's the answer?"

"I don't know! I don't, really! That's what makes it so fantastic."

The word brought a sweep of memory. "Fantastic" was the word Hugo had used to describe something that had gone on in this house. Her thoughts became jumbled. Hugo Bannister . . . the book . . . the suspicion of murder that hung over her . . .

She heard her voice burst out.

"It isn't only this—what's going on around here. I'm suspected of killing a man I would have no reason in the world to kill. His niece came to see me. She said dreadful things to me, accused me . . . And she's going to stay in the village until they make an arrest. I know she thinks I'm guilty!" Rosalie drew a long breath and waited until she had regained her composure. Then she said, "It's all mixed up somehow in that book Mr. Bannister was writing."

"I'm afraid," Richard said, "that you've lost me completely."

"That's not surprising. But maybe if you saw the book, too, you'd understand."

She turned away from him and went to the closet. She pushed aside the clothing hanging in it once more and found her suitcase. When she had unlocked it and put it on the bed, she took out the box with the manuscript in it.

It took her a little while to find the chapter with the heading, THE THAYERS, THE ALDRICHES AND THE MALEKALA.

"There," she said. "Read that," and she handed him the sheets of paper. She watched while his eyes traveled over the first one. When he had finished reading it, he looked up and said, "So old Aldrich married a native girl from a remote island. That wasn't so unusual in those days, was it? I seem to have heard that a number of sea captains brought back brides from far-off places. It's not unheard of now, either, among the boys in the service."

He studied the pallor and the bleakness of her face and then he put the manuscript aside. "Look," he said, "I don't have time to go all through this now. If you think there's anything here that would provide a motive for the author's death, then you should get in touch with the police right away. Didn't it occur to you that you should have done that right away?"

"Everything," she said, "everything piled up."

"I'll call Wellman for you, for this reason and because I don't like the idea of leaving you here alone with what's been going on."

"Now?" she asked. "You'll call him now?"

"Right this minute. There's a telephone downstairs. I'll do that and check back before I leave to tell you when he'll be here."

When he was gone, she put the manuscript in order and locked it away. Much as she wanted to read it, strong as was her desire to read the rest of the story about Ezra Thayer and his Saluan wife, she recognized the danger of allowing herself to become absorbed in it. It had taken Gloria's wild screaming to tear her out of the past when she had been reading the typewritten pages on that other occasion. She could not permit herself to fall into that spell again.

She had to remain aware, on her guard. She realized that the book represented something important. She did not yet know what it was but she was certain that the safest thing to do was to hide the manuscript lest someone come sneaking up on her and find her reading it. This time she might not be so lucky. The third attempt on her life might not fail.

Richard came back and said, "I was able to get in touch with Wellman. Technically, it isn't his case any longer. The state police have taken over. But when I explained that you were alone here and that I was sure you were telling the truth about those attacks on you, he promised to send someone over or come himself. I told him, too, that Mrs. Aldrich had died and that her great-granddaughter is missing."

"Thank you, Rosalie said, "for doing that but most of all for believing me."

There was about him already a look of detachment, an awareness of the need for hurrying to what awaited him in the hospital and the homes where people lay sick or in pain. He was a doctor again as he picked up his bag, his face absent and frowning. Out of the habit of accompanying the doctor, Rosalie walked with him to the door, and then she stopped short.

Realization swept over her. She would be alone. Completely alone. You could not count the dead woman nor the two servants who were here somewhere in this big, shadow-filled, silent house. She would have no one to turn to in case of need, in case the danger that had hovered over her ever since she had walked into this place, crept up on her and found her without defenses.

Night was even now falling, falling with the peculiar blackness that enveloped the sea and everything around it. A wind had sprung up and she could hear its low groaning against the window panes. Somewhere, far out on the ocean, a bellbuoy clanged its steady, dirgelike sound.

There arose from her constricted throat a frightened, mewling little sound and she felt rising throughout her body a cold shuddering. Her legs and knees grew weak and she could not have moved if her very existence depended on it. She stood there shivering and helpless with fear.

Richard stopped, too, and he came back to her. She knew that he must be able to see the whiteness and fear of her face because his own face changed. His free hand went out and he pulled her close to him and pressed her cheek against his shoulder.

He said, "Come on now, Nurse, the bogie man isn't going to get you," but there was no jeering in his voice, only a light tenderness, and the feel of his rough jacket against her skin was comforting. Some of his strength seemed to flow into her body and the shuddering grew weaker and finally stopped.

She stayed there without moving while his arm held her. She forced her emotions into control and made sure that she did not make the mistake she had made before. This time, she was determined, there would be no clutching or raising her head for his kisses. If she remained quiet and accepted his compassionate embrace for what it was, perhaps he would let it go on for a little while longer.

So I am willing to settle for crumbs, she told herself. I will be his friend or just another woman whose life his has touched intimately for a short time. I will take what he can give me: a smile, a kind word, even a twinkle of his eye. And what he gives me I will treasure and live on, remembering it and polishing it with dreams because it will be all that I will have of him.

Then I shall grow to be one of those sour, old-maid nurses who slowly become bitter because the dreams are worthless, who are feared and despised by patients and student nurses. I'll be one of those women whose love for a certain doctor is supposed to be a secret but is actually something to be laughed about and gossiped about; worst of all, I shall grow to be an object of pity.

Because I am in love with Richard.

13

THE SILENT AVOWAL brought only a feeling of resignation and heavy despair.

I will always be in love with him, she thought. There can never be any other man for me—never. He has spoiled for me anyone else I might meet and I shall die loving him. I am a great big fool, but that's the way it is and there's nothing I can do about it.

She could feel the uneven thudding of her heart but she remained there, quiet and unmoving, against his shoulder until he dropped his arm and stepped away.

"You'll be all right, dear," he said consolingly. "The sheriff or one of his men will be along before you know it."

She watched him leave the house, stood at the window waiting until the tall figure came out from under the overhang of the porch and ran down the steps and got into the car waiting in the driveway.

This is the way it will be for me from now on, she told herself. I will have to be satisfied with glimpses of him; I'll try to make excuses to see him, I'll lie in wait when I know he'll be at a certain place at a certain time. I'll try hard to keep it all out of my face when we meet, but I'll never be able to. He will know and other people will know, too. They'll laugh. Maybe he will, too.

Her insides felt sore, as though someone had reached into her body and pulled apart her heart and left it a torn and bleeding mass. And as though she would never in her life feel whole again.

I might as well get used to it, she said silently. It will go on for a long, long time.

There was nothing at all to do now except wait. There were not even the nursing duties to keep her occupied. The case was finished. She could do nothing for the woman who lay, her body a narrow ridge, under the sheet.

A knock at the door brought Rosalie springing out of her chair. She went to answer it cautiously. With her hand on the knob she called out, "Who's there?" and then when there came a mumbling, unintelligible answer from the other side, she opened the door a crack.

It was Azie who stood there, her eyeglasses glowing dimly as the light from the bedside lamp struck them. "Sorry," she muttered. "Sick today. But all right now. You want some dinner? Nobody else come."

"Later," Rosalie told her. "I'll be down later and get something. I'm waiting for a visitor now."

"Visitor, who?" The old woman stared boldly at her. "How she have visitors, her sick?" She peered around Rosalie into the room. "She better today? She not so sick as like before?"

Rosalie realized then that the servants had not been told of Mrs. Aldrich's death. She did not think that it was cause for personal grief as far as either Azie or Jug was concerned but when she spoke, it was with a certain gentleness, more out of respect for the woman who had been their mistress than out of consideration for the one who had worked in her kitchen.

"She passed away a little while ago," she said. "She was very old. She had lived for a long, long time. I do not know what Miss Aldrich will want from you. Perhaps she will close up this house when she marries. When she sees you, she will undoubtedly tell you."

The old woman seemed not to have heard the last part of what Rosalie said. She pushed herself into the room, her head thrust forward, and she stood staring at the covered figure on the bed. Her eyes were hidden behind the thick glasses and she looked like a figure carved of dark wood. Not a sound came through her lips.

After a while she ducked her head and backed away. Her footsteps were soft whispers on the carpet as she went down the hall. Then there fell over the death room a thick, heavy silence. It hung there like an ugly cloud.

A short time later it was broken, shattered by a wailing voice in the night. Hearing the voice, Rosalie thought at first that she must be imagining it, that the hush and the waiting in the room with the dead woman had affected her mind and was causing it to do tricks.

Then it came again and she realized that it came from somewhere outside the house and she heard what it was calling.

"Rosalie! Rosalie!"

Someone out there was crying her name. It came

again and again until her ears seemed to be filled with the sound. High and shrill it came. "Rosalie! Rosalie!" and she could detect the notes of desperation. Someone out in the night was appealing to her for help and she knew who that someone was. It could only be Gloria. The voice was the one that had screamed and wept here in this room that afternoon.

Rosalie went to the window and pushed back the draperies. She could see nothing except the blackness that hid the driveway and the lawn and the bushes around the house, the cliffs and the ocean beyond them.

The calling went on. "Rosalie, please! Oh, please!" The girl standing at the window could feel a shooting of chill up her spine and the tightening and prickling of her scalp. As she listened, the tone of the voice changed, grew weaker. "Help me! Rosalie, help me!" and then it petered off, as though Gloria had come to the end of her strength.

It was not possible to remain there any longer. Rosalie's mind was in turmoil. All that pressed through its agitation was the knowledge that Gloria was in some sort of mortal danger and that she, Rosalie, was the only one who could help her. And that she could not leave her alone in whatever danger threatened her there in the darkness of the night-shrouded grounds.

The wind, which had fallen, rose again. It moaned and groaned and shook the window panes. Its coldness seeped into the room. Rosalie, whose first impulse had been to dash outdoors, stopped when she was half-way to the door. She was in her uniform, chilled even now. She would have to get a coat and she went into the adjoining bedroom and pulled open the closet door.

Her coat was not hanging there.

She pawed through the dresses and her other uniforms, trying to remember where it was she had put the coat when she had moved her things from upstairs. Surely in this closet. There was no other. Panic sped her hands that pushed at the garments. There was no time for this. If she was to be of any help to Gloria, every moment counted.

I left it upstairs. I did not bring it down with my other clothes, she thought. It must be up there in the other room. I will have to go and see.

She was not thinking clearly. The need to find the coat absorbed her mind and she dashed out through the door that led to the hall, went running down the corridor. The light that she had turned on splashed long shadows against the walls. They were like living things lurking there in wait for her. She winced away from them, let out her breath in a gust of relief as she made the turn at the staircase landing. But then, if anything, it was even worse for the stairs leading up to the third floor were in almost total darkness.

Fear was like a sickness inside her and her heart was high and pounding and her lungs seemed to have swelled to the bursting point. There was a long string of doors along this hall, too, and she did not remember which one opened onto the room she had occupied for such a short time. She did not know whether or not she would be able to find it without long, time-wasting experimenting.

But she did, after only the second try, and she remembered where the light switch was on the wall. She snapped its button and the room sprang into light. She saw, pausing long enough to look around, that she was in the midst of a welter of disorder. Clothing was scattered on the chairs and on the bed. Odd shoes littered the floor. A jumble of underwear covered the top of the dresser. It looked as though Gloria had dumped things anywhere, everywhere, when she had moved her things from the room next to her great-grandmother's.

Rosalie's coat was not among the things in view nor was it in the closet. All that hung there were a couple of evening dresses and a jacket that evidently belonged to Gloria. It was a red-and-white plaid of some soft material, a little too gaudy for her taste and, she would have thought, for Gloria's.

She repeated to herself, grimly and half-aloud, the old saying about beggars being choosers while she snatched down the short coat and thrust her arms into its sleeves. Her good sense had come back and she realized that she had done a stupid thing in taking all this time to come upstairs to look for a coat instead of rushing out to help Gloria immediately.

Perhaps it was too late now and her haste would be futile but she ran, anyway, faster than she ever had in her life. Down the corridor, around the turn to the stairs, and there she almost fell. Only by clutching at the banister was she able to keep from plunging down the entire flight. Her narrow escape shook her composure again and questions kept beating at her mind. Would she be too late? Was Gloria already beyond help in some nameless horror out there in the blackness of the night?

So intent was she in making her way toward the first floor that she heard with ears that did not fully absorb them the waves of wailing that came muffled behind closed doors somewhere in the downstairs region of the house. Then, as they penetrated her brain, she stopped short.

Alternate waves of sobbing and wailing and crying out made a sound so horrible that she lifted her hands automatically and tried to close it out by covering her ears. But even then she could hear it too clearly, that dreadful dirgelike keening. It had a rhythmic cadence, like something in a nightmarish ritual, like nothing Rosalie had ever heard before.

Her hands fell to her side and she crept further down the stairs. From that point she could distinguish two voices. They rose in shrillness as they wailed and then fell to sobbing. There were words interspersed between the two sounds but they were unintelligible words, unfamiliar and strange, like those of a foreign language.

Rosalie stood there with her hand on the smooth surface of the banister, repelled by what was filling her ears, not wanting to go a step further but knowing that she must. Her first thought had been that it was Gloria who moaned and wept somewhere at the back of the house, but now she knew that that was not so. Neither of the voices sounded at all like Gloria's which had a light quality in it. Too, Gloria had been, Rosalie was sure, calling outside the house. If she had been able to come inside, wouldn't she have come upstairs looking for Rosalie?

A trick. Rosalie's mind moved to that possibility and seized on it. It must be some sort of trick to keep her from trying to find Gloria and helping her.

But it was not going to work. She was not going to fall into any sort of trap. Her purpose strengthened. Whatever was going on back there—in the kitchen, she thought—whoever was making those heinous sounds, she was not going to be frightened away from what she knew she had to do.

She closed her eyes as she started down the steps again because the sounds grew louder as she descended and they were so horrible, so eerie and soul-shaking, that she could scarcely endure hearing them. She moved to the wall and pressed her shoulder against it and in that position she slid down the remaining stairs.

The wailing stopped for a moment, changed to a steady chanting that had something weird and unearthly in its notes. And at that moment, Rosalie looked across the front hall and saw the front door looming at the other side of it.

She drew a long breath and began to run. The double doors to the drawing room were open and the dining room was dark and cavernous on the other side of her. She did not slow down to look into them but saw them from the corners of her eyes. All that she was aware of was the entrance door, only a few feet away from her now. Her eyes were riveted on it. All her energies were concentrated on reaching it.

Then, in a heart-stopping second, she realized that there was someone behind her. She became aware of a heavy fall of footsteps but she did not turn for she sensed the danger that was hurling itself upon her in the darkness of the hall. She lunged forward, her hands outstretched toward the door knob.

She missed it by inches.

There came from behind her, close to her ear, a deep grunt. Great, imprisoning arms wrapped themselves around her. She was pulled roughly backward, away from the entrance.

14

She was swept off her feet, as easily as though she were a rag doll. She felt herself lifted and slung over a rocklike shoulder. Her breath gone and too paralyzed at first to make any sound at all, she lay there with her head hanging down and her feet dangling.

Her hands were useless for there seemed to be no nerves in them but after that first moment of stunning shock, she found her fingers curling and making fists, and she began to beat upon the man's broad back.

Then her voice returned as she drew a long breath into her lungs. She screamed mindlessly, over and over again, until the hall was filled with the sound.

She was put down on her feet. The man slapped his hand over her mouth and holding her with his other viselike arm, he pushed her ahead of him along the hall beside the staircase and into the butler's pantry where, except for the faint shine of silver objects on the shelves, there was only darkness. Then he kicked open the door to the kitchen beyond which she could see a flickering light.

Because her breathing was cut off and because she was weak with such terror as she had never known in her life, her knees buckled and she slid out of the man's grasp and collapsed on the floor. Again he lifted her up effortlessly and carried her the rest of the way into the kitchen.

Her eyes were glazed with fear and at first she saw nothing except great, looming shadows. Then, when she was put on her feet again, her vision began to clear and the shadows took on outlines and became the huge stove, the long tables, the old-fashioned refrigerator with its headdress of coils. Candles, in tall holders, stood on one table and threw off an eerie, uneven light.

And she saw Azie.

The old woman stood by the stove and watched through her glittering eyeglasses while her son pushed toward her the wide-eyed girl who tottered on feet that felt like chunks of ice.

"There!" Azie ordered and pointed to a spot in the center of the worn linoleum. "She must stand there. We must do this now!"

Jug, his eyes on his mother's face, looked anxious and intent. He frowned, as though the effort of understanding what she said to him gave him pain. He pulled at Rosalie's arm and led her forward. Azie came slowly toward them and stopped when she was a foot away from them. She spoke sharply to the big man.

"Kneel!" she cried. "On your knees, my son! For she is your Malekala!"

Then they both went down on their knees, she moving laboriously and forced to steady herself with her hands. There at Rosalie's feet they began the chanting again. There was no moaning this time, just the sing-song rhythm of strange, foreign-sounding words that Rosalie could not identify.

Confusion immobilized her. She looked down at the two kneeling at her feet and swaying as they spoke and sang and she thought, It isn't real. It can't be! It is some sort of weird dream and I'll wake up in a little while and there won't be any of this—this craziness.

She began to back away, hoping that they were too engrossed in their strange ritual to notice her, but at the movement of her feet Azie raised her head and gestured to her son. He crawled away from her, got to his feet and lumbered to the door that led to the butler's pantry. He put himself in front of it and so Rosalie's only hope of escape was cut off.

Her head swiveled frantically. There were other doors in sight. One, she thought, probably led to the cellar but if she managed to reach that, she doubtlessly would not be able to find her way down dark, steep stairs at the bottom of which would lie a strange area. She would be trapped there.

Another door, at the other side of the room, might open onto the grounds at the rear of the house. Or to rooms that the servants occupied. It was an even chance but, in this unbelievable situation in which she found herself, the odds were not good enough.

Until she was certain that she could discover a way out of this incomprehensible nonsense, she would have to be wary.

It was not, she realized, nonsense to the two who had taken up their chanting again. Jug had fallen to his knees once more and he and Azie squatted with their bodies bent forward and uttered over and over syllables that did not seem to make the slightest bit of sense.

"Malekala!" they cried out at regular intervals and they would throw back their heads and look at Rosalie and then lean forward toward the floor until their foreheads nearly touched it. With their voices muffled, they poured out the stream of strange words and unfamiliar phrases.

There was not the slightest bit of use in trying to interrupt them, Rosalie knew. She stood clutching the plaid jacket around her shivering body, fighting for self-control now that the reaction after the assaults of terror had set in.

She tried to tell herself that they were crazy. That was it. For she had no other explanation for the lunatic actions. It was not only Jug, that hulking giant of a man, who was addle-brained. His mother, too, patently had some sort of mental abberation.

The ritual had evidently come to an end. Now they were struggling to get to their feet, Jug because of his size and his mother moving her old body painfully because, no doubt, age had made it brittle and arthritic.

Rosalie went to her and put out a hand. "Here, let me help you."

Azie cowered back. Her voice was shrill as she burst out, "No! No, Malekala does not touch unworthy flesh of Azie. Malekala, queen. Azie, nothing. A dog's spittle. Lower than the crawling insects. Not fit to touch!"

Rosalie could see the eyes behind their glasses gleaming wildly. The features in the dark-skinned face were distorted. And yet there was something—well, heroic about Azie. Rosalie, restored to some calmness by the simple act of offering help to the old woman, searched in her mind for a word to describe Azie. She looked exalted, that was it. Azie looked as though she were being transported by some sort of soul-lifting pride and happiness.

It did not seem menacing and Rosalie felt bold enough to say, "Look, Azie, why don't you tell me what this is all about? I don't understand why Jug brought me here, why you feel you have to kneel down in front of me. You called me by that strange name—Malekala. I am not, of course. I saw that word in a book that I've got upstairs. It said, and you said it too, that it means 'queen.' But I am not, of course I am not a queen of any sort at all. I'm Rosalie Dexter. I was Mrs. Aldrich's nurse."

Azie did not seem to be listening. She was backing away, bobbing her head and keeping her eyes down as she went.

"I am not!" Rosalie said more loudly. "It was the woman Captain Ezra Thayer married a long time ago, I think. The mother of Mrs. Aldrich, who just died. She was the one who was called . . .

Her voice grew thin and drifted away and she became dumb as a terrible knowledge burst in her brain. It was like a great white flare and she was blinded by it. The horror was back in full force now. She could not move nor even breathe. All she could do was stand there and stare at the old woman who reached into the burning coals of the big stove and took something from it. She held it in a steady hand, that long piece of iron with its glowing tip.

She began to walk slowly toward Rosalie.

A shriek burst from the girl's throat. "No!" she screamed. "Oh, Azie, no! You are wrong! I am not the Malekala!"

Azie's head moved in rhythm with the words she spoke. "Old Malekala dead. Young queen must wear the mark of the moon. Always Saluans must have queen. One dies, the next one who comes must show the world she still belong to us. No more big tribe." Her voice became sad. "Strangers come, take island.

"We cannot bring young Malekala anywhere for the festival, for this!" and she held out the branding iron as she walked closer to Rosalie. "So we must have ceremony here. Jug and me, still Saluans. Still must have a queen. So we come for you."

The glowing tip of the iron was thrust closer to Rosalie's face and she cringed away from it. She tried to back away but her feet felt rooted. There was a clamoring in her brain for now she knew. Now she understood so many things that had been incomprehensible before. As the old woman moved closer and closer to her, the things she had wondered about spun in her mind and took form and fell into place, and the dreadful picture was a complete one.

The book that Hugo had written with its chapter about Captain Thayer and his bride. The kidnaped daughter of an island queen. The mark of a crescent moon on the forehead of Zena Aldrich. The name of this house, Moontide. Gloria Aldrich's fear of the two servants. Her terror over the impending death of her great-grandmother.

Rosalie's throat felt closed over and she had to struggle to get her voice through it. When she gulped it out, it was a thin squeak. "You are making a mistake! I am not the Malekala, not the descendant of Zena Aldrich who is dead in her bedroom upstairs. Please listen to me! I am the nurse. You have seen me in the sickroom. You let me into this house. Look, I am still wearing my uniform!"

With palsied fingers, she tried to unbutton the jacket that belonged to Gloria, that distinctive red-and-white plaid garment that the servants had doubtlessly seen Gloria wearing dozens of times. Azie, who was half blind, and Jug, who had the mind of a small child, had mistaken one girl for the other. How easy that would have been to do when they resembled each other so closely and Gloria had taken to arranging her hair like Rosalie's.

She must tell them. She had to make them see that they had made a mistake.

Her fingers fell away from the buttons of the jacket. She realized that if she convinced them of the truth she would be only shifting the horror away from herself to Gloria. They would go searching for the real descendant of Minita Thayer, daughter of a Saluan queen, and possibly find her.

It was possible that they had already had her in their possession earlier this evening.

That was it. That was the way it had been. Rosalie was certain of it. They had taken Gloria away as soon as they had learned of her great-grandmother's death and she had found some way to escape from them. She had called to Rosalie to help her keep out of their clutches and Rosalie had tried to go to her. Jug, seeing her there in the dark hall, had seized her, thinking that he had Gloria once more. In the kitchen with its flickering candlelight, poor half-blind Azie wouldn't have been able to distinguish one girl from another.

All these things flashed through Rosalie's mind. And she knew that she could not go on trying to convince Azie of her true identity. For by saving herself she would condemn the other girl to this bizarre horror. And, she thought, if Gloria had found a way to escape so could she.

The question was—how?

Azie had stopped a few feet away from her and was mumbling to herself. Now she fell silent and began to move toward Rosalie again and the branding iron with its burning tip in the shape of a crescent was in clear view.

Rosalie drew breath into her lungs swiftly and cried out in a voice that she hoped she made sound imperious, "Not now! Not yet!"

Out of surprise, Azie halted. Jug moved away from the door to the butler's pantry and Rosalie saw, from the corner of her eye, the shadow of his great body moving in the light from the candles.

"We must not do it this way," she said, lifting her chin high. Her imagination had become honed in her desperation and her brain had never moved more swiftly. What would a native queen say, do, in these circumstances? How would she speak to her subjects? In what manner would she postpone the physical agony of an old ritual? Rosalie cried, "We must pray!"

She saw Azie's head drop in an attitude of submission and she went on, "We must pray to our moon goddess. It is she who rules over us, isn't that so? She is benevolent as well as just, and we must ask her to guide me so that I may rule my people wisely. I will not accept the mark of Malekala until I speak to her tonight."

She heard her own voice but she could not believe that she was actually saying these idiotic things, talking about moon goddesses and her "people." Putting on a regal, lunatic act in this place only a few miles from civilization. Standing here in a kitchen lighted only by a flickering candle where a dark woman waited to burn her forehead in a long-forgotten savage ritual.

It must be some sort of weird nightmare. Surely she would awaken at any minute to find herself in her own home.

It was no bad dream. It was real, and unless she was able to outwit this old woman with the branding iron in her hand, she would carry to her death, as Zena Aldrich had done, an ugly scar on her forehead. And after the branding was done, what would they do to her then? Would they allow her to escape or would they keep her captive in some remote place where she would never be found again?

She would have to go on acting the queen as a delaying tactic until she could figure out a way to get out of this horrible kitchen.

Staring into Azie's face, she said, "We will pray to the moon goddess," and the old woman nodded. But when Rosalie took a tentative step toward the door, Jug moved in her direction and stood close to her, his big body looming over her.

"Yes, pray," she said again. "But we must do it outside where we can look upon her in all her beauty and she can see us on our knees and know that we are worshiping her, that we are her subjects."

She thought, for a moment, that it was going to work and a great surge of hope rose inside her. She was sure that she had won when Azie bent her head even farther, as though in obedience to a royal dictum. But then, surprisingly, Jug spoke. Rosalie had never heard him do anything much more than grunt a syllable or two before this. The sound of his voice made her start.

"She did not come out tonight. Moon goddess lost to us behind the clouds in the sky. I looked for her. She not to be seen."

Rosalie's hope died, smothered under a great weight of despair. She cried shrilly, "But she is never far from us! No matter where she is, she watches us. So let us do it here. Before you put the mark on me, I must speak to her. How could I be a good Malekala without that?"

She raised her hand with the palm held out. "Come, we shall kneel right here on the floor and you, my subjects, will say the words. Because I do not know them, I have never been taught the language of my forefathers. Speak, Azie and Jug, speak to our moon goddess!"

Raising both arms, she sank to her knees and

bent her body forward. When she lifted her eyes, she saw Azie making the painful trip to the floor. Then, as his mother gestured, Jug knelt, too.

They began again the chanting and Rosalie knew that if there was ever to be a moment this was it. The two were absorbed in their praying. With fervent voices and enraptured faces, they were lost to the real world around them. It would take them a little while to return to it.

That was Rosalie's advantage. And she was young, her body was disciplined. She could pull herself up, move, turn, run for the door before they could wrench themselves back to reality and struggle to their feet again.

She moved swiftly and they were caught by surprise when, in a single movement, she lifted herself up, then skirted around Jug and plunged toward the door to the butler's pantry. She heard the gasping of their voices and the shuffling of their feet as they tried to get up.

Her own footsteps echoed as she ran across the kitchen with her hand thrust out in front of her. She pressed it hard against the door which opened easily and then swung back into place behind her. Their voices followed her, Azie's high and agonized, Jug's a loud grunt.

"Hurry! Go find her! She must come back!"

It was Azie who cried out, and Rosalie knew that it would be only a matter of seconds before the big, lumbering man would be after her. His strides would be long. He would know this dark hall better than she could. And he had great, reaching arms that could capture her easily and hold her so strongly that there would be no possibility of escaping from them. This time she would have no chance of getting away.

Her only hope was to get to the front door before he overtook her. She could hear his footsteps pounding behind her now, and she could not run any faster because the paralysis of her fear was beginning to overwhelm her again and her legs were growing weak with it and she felt herself stumbling.

She came out of the pantry and she could see, through the gloom of the front hall, the big entrance door. It seemed miles away and she was certain that she would never reach it in time. Then a fresh wave of terror swept over her as a new, dreadful thought thrust itself into her mind.

The front door might be locked.

That possibility had not occurred to her before. And she knew that if she could not get the door open, if she had to stand there and pull at the knob, grope for the latch or the bolt that lay across it, she was lost. The time she spent fumbling would be time enough for Jug to reach her. Then he would drag her back into the kitchen. Having learned their lesson, Azie and Jug would not give her another opportunity for trickery. The burning brand would be put on her forehead immediately.

Rosalie went rushing across the hall, summoning up every bit of strength she possessed and with speed she had not believed she was capable of; and she threw herself against the door. Because there was not enough light by which to see very much, she slid her hand along it until she found the knob. She wrenched at it and it moved under her fingers. Her breath came out in a sob of relief. The door was open.

She pulled it to her and the night air rushed in on her, and she thought that she had never known anything so wonderful as the feeling of it on her face. Even the blackness outside, the lashing wind, the sound of the ocean, were welcome after the horror she had just left. Although she could see nothing in front of her, she ran forward and then slowed down when she thought she must be close to the top step. For she realized that a fall now would be calamitous.

She heard Jug's footsteps come banging through the door and onto the boards of the porch. And she heard his heavy grunting and she could imagine his hands reaching out behind her. Her toe found the top step and she went down that one and then the others. She came onto the driveway and she ran blindly out into the night.

The ground clam shells crunched under her feet and she knew that she had to get on the grass so that her pursuer could not follow the sound of her running. But she did not know which way to go, could not decide in that split-second of panic whether to take a chance on trying to hide in the bushes that surrounded the house or to try to head for the path that led away from Moontide in the direction of the village.

She knew that she would not get very far along the path. She was tiring. Her lungs ached and her throat burned. She could not go on trying to keep distance between her and Jug. She would collapse if she went much further.

The carriage house came into her thoughts for

a moment. She had made the turn at the driveway and was on the footpath now that led to the little building at the rear of the house. She could see it looming, its outlines dark against the lighter sky, and in that instant she let herself think that it might be a haven. But she could see no light coming from there; the door of it was evidently closed. And even if she reached it, and tried to barricade herself into it, there would be no time to keep Jug out and she could remember, all too clearly, the awful few minutes she had spent in there. The remembered horror made her stagger and she caught at a bush to keep herself from falling.

Jug was thrashing about, she could hear that. With the noise of the tide and her own harsh breathing, she heard nothing else. Not the car coming up the path beside her. When she saw the sweep of the headlights, she stopped because they blinded her. They fell upon her, so that she seemed to be in the center of a spotlight's rays, as the car made the turn in the driveway.

The dazzlement faded from her eyes and she saw the figure running, like some poor, dazed animal, directly into the path of the car. She tried to cry out, knowing that it was Jug, knowing that his undeveloped brain had room for only one thing at a time and that he was so intent on chasing after her that he had not even been aware of the car bearing down on him.

The brakes squealed. The tires made a whirring sound as they stopped abruptly. Jug's thick voice made a single protesting shout. And then was still.

15

THERE WAS THAT moment of hush. The whole world seemed to be wrapped in it for only a moment out of time. And then came the screaming—the wild, animal-like shrieks. Azie came tottering into the brightness, her mouth snapping open and shut, her arms lifting and falling in frantic gestures. Little as she was able to see, she seemed to know, by some instinct, that the big, fallen body silhouetted in the brilliance of the headlights was that of her son and that life was leaving him. She threw herself across him and she lay there, wailing with shrill, wordless cries.

Rosalie stood with frozen hands clutching the jacket around her. The wind, sweeping up from the water, was sharp; but the chill came from deep inside her and it spread waves of iciness through her until she was shivering with such force that she felt ill. Everything around her began to spin in swirls of darkness. She was caught up in them, whirled about, felt herself fainting.

Somebody came to her side and grabbed her as she was falling. And after that, for a long time, there was nothing but a confusion that was like a series of dreams without sequence.

She was taken into the house. She was placed on the old sofa in the back parlor. She could feel the stiffness of the plush upholstery against her scalp for the numbness of her senses was beginning to wear off and they were becoming sensitive and acute.

The musty smell of the room's furniture was strong in her nostrils. From the front of the house she could hear voices and sounds of activity. Then the noise of the footsteps of people, several of them it seemed, moved into the hall and up and down the stairs.

She was thoroughly conscious again and the memory of everything that had happened came pouring back and there formed in her mind pictures so hideous that she had to close her eyes to shut them out.

Exhaustion overcame her and there was another interval of sleeping or letting her brain be numbed. She did not know which nor did she have any idea how long she lay there. When she awoke, she felt alert again. She opened her eyes to find Sheriff Wellman sitting beside her.

There was a man with him, a stocky, moonfaced man who wore a gray suit and his prematurely gray hair in a careful pompadour. His name, the sheriff said, was Lieutenant Callahan. She thought he added, "State Policc," but was not sure. The lieutenant did not look like a policeman.

After the introductions were over, Rosalie turned her head and saw that Richard Sargent had came into the room. He was standing beside a piecrust table that held his bag and he was looking at her with a professional, critical gaze.

She tried to struggle up into a sitting position and she said indignantly, "But I'm all right. I don't need a doctor." and then she sank back, blushing.

It was always this way. She seemed to lose her head when Richard was around. Because he was there with his bag, it did not necessarily mean that he had come on her account. A man had been killed on the driveway a short time ago. How long? She did not know when it had been. Enough time had passed, evidently, for a doctor to have been summoned and to have arrived and made the pronouncement.

He moved closer to the sofa and looked down at her with a frown that might have come from worry about her (there was no harm in letting herself dream for an instant) or because someone had been killed needlessly or because his busy schedule had been interrupted once more.

At any rate, he went on standing there when Sheriff Wellman said, "We want you to tell us exactly what happened here tonight, Miss Dexter."

Richard put in, "If you're sure you're up to it, Rosalie. If you want to rest a little longer . . ."

She shook her head. She wanted to get it all said, to tell of the horror and so, perhaps, exorcise it. When she began to speak, her voice was halting because she did not expect any of them to believe the events of the night.

How could she hope that they would believe she had actually been dragged into that cavernous kitchen with its flickering candles and missed, by only the barest of margins, having the brand of the Malekala of Salua burned into her forehead?

"You know, you saw it on Mrs. Aldrich," she appealed to Richard when she had finished telling that part of it. "That was what the scar was, the mark of the crescent moon. Because they worshiped the moon goddess. The Saluans did. The tribe of natives who lived on an island where the owner of this house once stopped. The daughter of the Saluan queen was the wife of that man," she finished lamely, knowing that the more she talked the more fantastic what she was saying sounded.

"Fantastic," she said aloud. "That was how Hugo Bannister described something that went on in this house, the secret of the Thayers and the Aldriches."

When she spoke Hugo Bannister's name, the expressions on the faces of the two law officers seemed to change. Almost imperceptibly, they leaned closer to her.

"It's in his book." She was growing weary again. She did not see how she could summon up enough strength to go on with the explanation and when she tried to remember the exact words in that important chapter of the book, her head began to ache. She lifted a hand and touched it gingerly.

"You can read it for yourselves," she said. "It'll all be in the book. I have it locked in my suitcase. And the key to that is in my handbag that I left in the bedroom next to Mrs. Aldrich's. You'll find the suitcase in the closet there."

Richard offered, "I'll show you."

The three men went out of the room and after a while Richard came back alone.

"They're reading it now," he said and sat down beside her in the chair the sheriff had been occupying. He picked up her hand and felt her pulse. It seemed to take him a long time, much longer than was necessary, and even when he had finished, he did not release her wrist. His fingers slid around it and then moved down and gathered up hers.

"Rosalie," he said, without quite looking at her, "I'm sorry I was such a blind, deaf, dumb idiot. You tried to tell me all that and I thought—heck, I don't know what it was I thought. It seemed to me . . . Well, we won't talk about it any more now. I've got an idea you're going to have to go over it and over it, you poor kid! When those two come back. And at the inquest. And probably for reporters if they get to you. So just lie there and take it easy now."

How could she? How could she be quiet and calm when he was there so close to her, his face concerned, his hand holding her gently? Of course he must have felt the unevenness of her pulse when he touched it; she was certain that he must be aware of the throbbing of her fingertips. But nothing showed in his expression except solicitude.

I might be his patient, she thought with a touch of bitterness and she refused sharply when he spoke of giving her a sedative. She wanted to be alert for the next session with Sheriff Wellman and the lieutenant of the state police. Besides, there was something that kept fluttering to the edge of her mind and tantalizing her and then fluttering away again. It was something she should know or think of; it was a vague, nagging feeling that there was something she should be doing or telling someone about. She would never be able to pin it down if her mind was drugged with medicine.

When the two men came back, they were grim-faced. But she could detect a subtle change in their manner toward her. When they had settled themselves on chairs again, they asked her deferentially to resume her story, and she had the impression that anything she said now would be accepted as the truth.

"You've told us about what happened in the kitchen," the sheriff said. "Now go ahead and tell us the rest of it. Don't leave anything out."

She began, "Well, he came out of the house after me and I knew I had to get away from him but I didn't know which way to run," but the sheriff waved his hand impatiently. "You can skip that part. We know. It was my car that hit him. Technically, I'm guilty of vehicular manslaughter and there's that to clear up, too. There was no way, no way at all, of avoiding him. He ran right in front of the car.

"No, what I mean is, go way back. Right from the start. To the time when you were staying at Hugo Bannister's house."

"But Mr. Bannister and his dying had nothing at all to do with this!" Surprise made her voice sound shrill in the small, crowded room. "I only suggested that you look at the book he had been writing so you would understand about Ezra Thayer's wife and why Zena Aldrich was branded with a crescent moon and why Azie and Jug, thinking that I was Gloria, tried to brand me. That was the only reason."

As she spoke Gloria's name, her voice began to

peter out. She knew now what it was her mind hadn't been able to capture. In her engrossment with Jug's death and her own collapse and then being alone with Richard with something between them that had never been there before, thoughts of Gloria had been lost somewhere but now she said the girl's name aloud.

"Please!" Sheriff Wellman had become impatient again. "Tell us about Mr. Bannister."

She tried. She spoke about the death of the man who had been her patient, how it had been attributed to a heart attack and how incredulous she had felt when she had learned that he had died by poisoning.

After he had died, she told them, she had come here to Moontide to nurse the dying Mrs. Aldrich. "Doctor Sargent asked especially that I be on the case," she said, and she saw Richard's head come up and the blank look that swept over his face. "And somebody tried twice to kill me. I told you that. And that I did not have any idea why and still haven't."

She described the events of the hours just past, how she had heard Gloria calling to her and rushed about to try to go to the girl, how she had found her own coat gone and borrowed the jacket that belonged to Gloria.

"And Jug saw me going through the hall. They thought I was Gloria, Azie not being able to see very well and Jug not all that bright. They made that mistake. And that's the way it was," she finished. "Everything just as I told you, how I got away from them and all."

"Not quite." Lieutenant Callahan shook his head. "It's not the whole story."

Rosalie swung her head around and looked at him. Then she moved her glance to the sheriff.

"You better explain it to her," he said. "She still doesn't understand."

"The two are connected," Lieutenant Callahan told her. "Hugo Bannister's murder and what's been happening here. What we're doing is trying to prevent another killing. That's what this is all about."

Her lips felt numb for a moment and then she burst out, "Gloria! That's what I tried to tell you. She was absolutely terrified. She must have known, of course, that once her great-grandmother was dead, Azie and Jug would consider her the new Malekala and force the brand on her. She was afraid of them, and now I can understand why.

"But they were being used—I know that's true! It was her step-sister who manipulated them because she wanted Gloria dead. So that she—Julie Merrick—could get the estate and marry the man they were both in love with!"

She had to stop for breath then. She had to stop and try to control her voice so that when she resumed speaking, she could tell them more calmly about the threat she had heard Julie making.

"Don't you see?" she asked. "She had to wait until after Mrs. Aldrich died to get the money. Then she intended to do away with Gloria. Perhaps with the help of the two servants or perhaps alone. But somehow."

Then her voice rose and she shouted at them, "Gloria is missing! She cried out to me and asked me to help her. And I tried—oh, I did try! You must believe me! That's why I got her jacket and went downstairs—because she was outside somewhere in the darkness calling to me. I don't know how I could have forgotten that! I should have told you about Gloria before anything else. All this time wasted! It may be—it may be too late now!"

The two men had stiffened, as though obeying some silent call to attention. She saw them exchange glances. Sheriff Wellman said sternly, "You're right, Miss Dexter. You should have told us this right away," and she nodded.

She choked remorsefully, "I'm very sorry. But everything was so terribly confused. I wasn't thinking straight. It wasn't that I forgot exactly but just that it got pushed to the back of my mind. So much time has passed now. I'll never forgive myself if anything has happened to her!"

They were not listening. They had come up out of their chairs, snatched up their hats and were on their way to the door. As she was struggling off the sofa, the sheriff turned and asked, "You're sure you searched the entire house?"

"As much as I was able. When I was looking for Julie, that is. There are so many rooms that are hidden in ells and additions and it would have taken me all night to go into all of them. She is not in the house, I feel sure of that. She was calling to me from outside."

She was babbling and she could not seem to stop. The compulsion to pour out all her fears and distress overpowered her. "The grounds are so big," she cried, her teeth chattering; for she could feel it all again, the desperation and the panic, turning this way and that as she tried to find a hiding place, the moment of indecision when she did not know whether to try to conceal herself in the bushes, make a run for it down the path or dash for the carriage house . . .

"The carriage house!" she cried so loudly that the lieutenant stopped with his hand on the door knob and Sheriff Wellman turned back again and looked at her. They asked in chorus, "What did you say?"

She went closer to them. "I just remembered about the coach house. It was in there that somebody tried to kill me. If that's where Gloria was taken, she would not—would not have a chance to escape."

They had heard enough and they did not remain to hear any more. They went through the door and the sound of their footsteps pounded along the hall beyond. Rosalie evaded Richard's outstretched hand and went after them, following the twin beams of their flashlights that shot streaks of light ahead of them.

She ran as fast as she could but Richard overtook her.

"You've had enough," he panted. "You want to collapse again?"

He tried to stop her but she wrenched herself out of his grasp and ran through the open door, guided by the brightness of the policemen's torches. The moon had broken through the clouds and it shed pale light over the driveway.

There were two or three cars there; she did not stop to count. The vehicle that had taken Jug's body away, and doubtlessly Azie accompanying it, was gone. In one of the police cars a radio squawked, unheeded.

Rosalie ran across the driveway to the footpath and then stopped. In the light of the moon, she could see the carriage house and the two men who had stopped in front of the closed double doors.

They were pounding on them but the sound of it was drowned out by their shouting voices. The pounding and the calling went on for only a little while, stopped before Rosalie and Richard reached them. When he turned and saw them coming, the sheriff ordered, "Stand back!"

He began to thrash among the bushes and the grass and finally motioned to Lieutenant Callahan. They bent and then straightened up carrying a log between them. They made a battering ram of it and smashed it again and again against the door.

After repeated assaults, there came the noise of wood shattering and they let the log fall to the ground. Sheriff Wellman thrust his hand in through the hole they had made and his body moved back and forth until he found what he was looking for, a bolt or a lock on the other side of the door. He pushed it open and the two men disappeared through it.

Rosalie felt Richard's arm around her as he held her there on the narrow path. She could scarcely bear the waiting. Her heartbeats were rapid and her breathing was loud. She was certain of what she would see when the two law officers came out of the coach house again. She was certain that one of them would be carrying the body of another murder victim but she was unable to tear her eyes away from that spot of yawning darkness.

She heard the sound of movement from inside the barn and they both came out, one behind the other. And each carried a limp body in his arms. She and Richard stepped back off the path to let them pass and she looked down first at Gloria whom the lieutenant bore easily and then at Julie Merrick whose weight seemed to stagger Sheriff Wellman.

Without speaking, she and Richard hurried along behind the little procession. At a cleared spot where the lawn bordered on the driveway, the two men stopped and put their burdens down side by side.

Lieutenant Callahan took his torch from his pocket and in the rays from that and the light of the moon, Rosalie could see that the skin of both the girls' faces was bright red, as though from scalding. Their eyes were closed and at first they seemed not to be breathing. But when Richard knelt beside them and put his ear first to the chest of one and then the other, he made a reassuring signal. He looked up and said, "They're alive. But we're going to have to get them to the hospital."

Sheriff Wellman started toward the house but the lieutenant stopped him. "You disconnect that thing in there?"

"I did." The voices of the two men were gritty with grimness. "It's a lucky thing we got there in time. Another few minutes and they'd both be gone."

He had turned and looked down at Gloria and at that moment her eyelids began to flicker. They all waited, nobody moving, no one speaking, until her eyes opened wide. They were glazed and expressionless then but after ten seconds or so, a wild light came into them and she tried to struggle up into a sitting position. Her hand went to her throat and she whimpered. As she was sinking back onto the ground, she became aware of the girl beside her. She pulled herself forward and away, and she began to sob.

Her hand moved as though there were weights at the ends of her fingers and she pointed at the unconscious girl beside her.

"She tried to kill me!" she croaked.

16

RICHARD WAS on his feet. He said, "I'll be right back," and rushed into the house. He came back in an incredibly short time carrying his black bag. No one had spoken after Gloria's outburst. She lay weeping, her voice becoming louder with each sob. Lieutenant Callahan said to Richard, as he motioned to Julie, "She seems to have got the worst of it. This one's going to make it all right."

His tone was so harsh that Rosalie turned to stare indignantly at him. She had wanted to go to Gloria during Richard's short absence but the lieutenant had waved her back and she had been puzzled then. But now she was angry and her voice, when she spoke to him, was sharp.

"She must be feeling pretty bad. She needs attention, too. At least I can hold her hand, let her know that somebody . . ."

It was the sheriff who motioned her away this time. He had come out of the house behind Richard, muttering something about the ambulance being there soon. Now he stood beside Rosalie and she could see the sternness in his tight features and the cold look in his eyes as he studied Gloria.

What was the matter with the two men? Rosalie wondered. She was bewildered by their attitude toward the victim of a near murder, a poor child who had narrowly escaped death. Surely Gloria needed comforting after her ordeal in the coach house. She must be wrackingly sick at this moment from, Rosalie was able to guess, monoxide poisoning. Surely she deserved to be treated with more sympathy and consideration.

Rosalie shook off the restraining hand and pushed forward as the lieutenant reached down and pulled the girl to her feet. He said, "All right, suppose you tell it the way it really was. You want to do that?"

Gloria's eyes were big. The bright color was fading from her face and it looked white and sickly in the moonlight. Her lips moved stiffly and she said, "She tried to kill me. Julie tried to murder me with monoxide poison."

Rosalie felt dazed. She looked from one to the other as Sheriff Wellman said, "You can't question her here, Ed."

The lieutenant nodded. "You're right. Okay, Miss Aldrich, you've got your rights. You don't have to answer my questions without your attorney being there. You can call one when we get to the barracks. Tell him you're being held for murder."

Richard, who was squatting beside Julie, looked up at the instant Rosalie's head swiveled in his direction. Their lips moved in unison. "Murder!"

Gloria stood as still as though she had been carved out of stone, a slim, white marble statue with sightless eyes. Her rigid body seemed as though it would never move again, and then suddenly it began to sag and sink slowly toward the ground.

But Gloria was not in a state of collapse. Her

movement had been a calculated one to catch the two law officers off guard. As she bent her knees, she slid under the lieutenant's arm and pulled away from his reaching hand.

She made an arc around him and began to run, blindly and with her head down in heedless flight. Rosalie, who had been standing behind the lieutenant and to the rear of him, moved by instinct only—she did not think nor plan it—into Gloria's path.

The impact of the girl's body sent her breath rushing out in a great gasp. She went reeling backward and her arms, thrown out to grab at something to keep her from falling, went around Gloria's body. The two girls went down together and Gloria, like some wild, fear-crazed animal, began to pound and scratch in a whirlwind of fury until Rosalie felt her face becoming bruised from the blows and then stinging from the sharp fingernails that dug into it.

Gloria was being tugged at her during the assault, shouted at (Rosalie could hear Richard's voice above those of the others) was captured and lost as she bit and screamed and kicked. It took the three men to pull her off Rosalie and even then her arms and legs were flailing and her head thrashed and there poured from her throat curses and obscenities.

Rosalie lay stunned. It was the words and phrases that Gloria was shrieking that kept her paralyzed in shock. Her face stung, she could feel the dribble of blood on it. Her scalp was still sore from the hair-pulling and her jaw ached where it had been pounded. But it was Gloria's screaming out filth and blasphemy that kept Rosalie locked in this daze of seeming unreality.

Even while she was being held between the two men, Gloria tried to lunge at the other girl. "You!" she screeched. "It was you that spoiled everything!"

In her struggle to get free, her head fell forward and swayed from side to side and her hair swung over her face. Then she threw herself backward and her screams became a wild, unrestrained sobbing. Suddenly she became limp, her knees buckling. Only the lieutenant held her now and he half-carried, half-pushed her toward one of the cars in the driveway.

Rosalie felt Richard's arms around her and she heard the sheriff's voice, as though coming from a long way off, say, "Better take that one into the house, Doctor. I'll wait here for the ambulance, let you know when it gets here. Better give her a pill or something and take care of those scratches."

It was like something in a dream, being taken into the house again, back to the sofa in the small parlor, feeling Richard's hand around hers as she held the glass of water and swallowed the pill he gave her, hardly aware of the smarting of her skin as he daubed at her face.

She heard the ambulance's siren and then Richard went away for a little while. When he came back, the sheriff was with him. By that time life seemed to have returned to her body. There were things she wanted to say, questions she had to ask.

But Richard would not permit it. "You can get your deposition tomorrow," he told Sheriff Wellman, "I'm taking her home now," and when Rosalie mumbled something about her own car, he said, "No problem. It can stay here tonight and I'll drive you back tomorrow to pick it up. That can wait, too."

There were no more arguments. He had spoken. "My lord and master," she murmured under her breath so that he would not hear.

17

He would not even let her go upstairs for her clothing and her suitcase. "Don't get yourself worked up about trivia. When you come to get your car, you can take care of all that."

Not tomorrow, not ever, did she want to return to Moontide, but Richard was being officious and seemed to be enjoying it so she let him take charge of everything. When she was in his car, beside him in the front seat, he said, "No talking now," so she remained silent. It was enough to merely sit there, her head resting against the back of the seat. She tried, although she did not quite succeed, to forget everything, to pretend that none of it had happened.

When they reached her house and her mother saw her battered face, Richard almost had another patient on his hands.

"I've said it over and over!" Mrs. Dexter wailed. "She should have picked some nice, safe profession. Like teaching school."

She did not smile when he said, "Safe? These days?" and she became diverted by a different kind of worry when she noticed the way he was looking at her daughter.

He ordered, "Get to bed, honey. I'll be back in the morning."

It was fairly early when he came. Lieutenant

Callahan arrived minutes later with a young trooper from the state police who carried a portable stenotype machine and settled himself in a corner. Rosalie was conscious of his flying fingers while she talked.

Once again she recounted everything she knew. When she had finished, she asked, "What will happen to her—Gloria, I mean? And Julie, where is she?"

Julie, Richard said, was in the hospital. "She got a bad dose of the monoxide. But she's going to be all right. Gloria's in jail, I guess."

The lieutenant nodded. "She's been booked. Murder One. No bail. Pretty as she is, I doubt she'll be able to convince a jury of her innocence. Say," he exclaimed, staring at Rosalie, "she does look a lot like you!"

They were in the living room. Everything was familiar: the good, slightly worn furniture and the imitation Oriental rug and the fireplace mantle with its clock and her pictures on it. The photographs were a history of her life; they showed her as a baby, a high school graduate, a nurse in her new "whites." It seemed far removed from Moontide and its horrors, from death and violent passions.

Rosalie said faintly, "She did kill him then? She murdered Hugo Bannister?"

"She did indeed."

Lieutenant Callahan nodded to the young trooper who left the room. Rosalie was sitting in a chair that faced a window and she could see the two-toned car in front of the house. The officer got into it, slid behind the wheel and leaned forward to listen to the squawking radio. She thought the lieutenant, too, would be leaving at any minute and she said, "Please tell me the rest of it."

"What else is there? It was premeditated murder. That's why she killed him—the book he was writing. No, actually, I guess it went further back than that, to the old sea captain who kidnaped a savage girl."

"Savage?"

"Exactly. That's what Minita Thayer was. We read part of the book. Enough. When you think of the South Sea islands, you imagine Tahiti. You think of friendly, easy-going, brown-skinned natives smiling and playing guitars and singing and making things out of sea shells. At least I do—I did," he amended. "The Saluans weren't that kind of people. Not at all. They were what I said—savages. Warlike. Clinging to atavistic rites. No missionary would have dared to set foot on their island. He would have been tortured to death—to say the very least."

Rosalie asked, "But Captain Thayer?"

"According to Bannister's book, some of his crew members were killed by the Saluans. The ship was armed and he managed to defend himself and the remaining men. Then he struck some sort of bargain with the chieftains. Gunpowder, or something like that, for amnesty while the ship was repaired. It was during the layover that old Ezra saw the queen's daughter and coveted her.

"It was quite a story. The night they were to sail, Ezra sent a couple of his men out to kidnap the young girl. And he brought her back here and built the house for her. It must have seemed like a prison to her for she never left it. No one ever saw her and he must have bribed or threatened his men because Minita was never gossiped about.

"Anyone seeing her would have been surprised—well, I guess the word is shocked. Because the Saluans, as I said, were not gentle, brown-skinned people. There were savage blacks. It's a pretty good bet that Minita was black, too."

Rosalie shook her head and said on a whispering sigh, "I feel as though I'm listening to some improbable adventure story."

"You haven't heard the whole of it yet." The lieutenant smiled at her. "Minita and Ezra had only the one daughter—Zena Aldrich. And when her mother died, that made Zena the crown princess of the Saluans. Somehow they discovered where she was. They sent a couple of the tribe members to Moontide and Zena was spirited away. We don't know just where she was taken—Bannister evidently never learned that. Perhaps it was to Salua they took her and branded her and tried to persuade her to rule them. Or maybe it was somewhere closer where a colony of them had settled. Anyway, she must have escaped from them or else she was so unhappy—a girl brought up in a place like Stoneport would have been miserable in tribal existence—that they released her. Now the Saluans are gone, except for a few descendants of the tribe. The island was taken over and civilized more than fifty years ago. Azie and Jug are evidently members of a small group that clung together, went on practicing the old customs and rituals, kept track of the woman they considered their queen.

"We don't know where they came from, those two," he said. "We can only guess that they learned of Zena Aldrich's serious illness and wanted to be near Gloria who, to them, would be the new Malekala. They would have had nowhere to take her and that's why the branding was to have taken place here."

Richard turned to look at Rosalie, concerned about how the mentioning of the brand had affected her. She managed to smile at him and he asked the lieutenant, "You mean to say you got all that from Bannister's book? And where did he get it?"

"From Gloria's father. The two were close friends. The book is dedicated to Philip Aldrich. That chapter of it, with that old story of the sea captain and the Malekala's daughter, would have made the book. It would have caused a sensation. Maybe even made a movie."

"What I cannot see," Rosalie put in, "is why Gloria's father would reveal all that, permit such a story about his own family to be published."

The twist of the lieutenant's mouth was cynical. "The magic word is money. The Aldrich fortune was depleted. Bad investments, maybe. High taxes or high living. Philip Aldrich was quite a swinger, as we say in these days. He was hoping to recoup the fortune from his share of the book. We don't know how Gloria found out about it. Maybe she came across some notes or letters between him and Bannister. Maybe Bannister wanted to be fair and offered her her father's share of the profits.

"But I guess she had other ideas about how to get her hands on some money. And if Bannister refused to give up the idea of having the manuscript published when she begged him to, she would have been desperate. Desperate enough to visit her father's old friend with a bottle of poisoned wine and lying offers of friendship on her lips."

"You said she had other ideas about how to get money." Richard glanced over at Rosalie who stared back at him levelly. "You mean Chandler? She was expecting to marry him. She wasn't going to let anything stand in the way of that?"

"Exactly. Eventually he might have learned about it. Couldn't very well help it, after they were married. But she would have put herself in the way of a good, big, fat divorce settlement. The Chandlers are family proud. They wouldn't have wanted a scandal. Of course he wouldn't have married her if he had known, allowed that difference in the Chandler blood line."

Rosalie was murmuring, half to herself. "There was no money. That's plain enough now. Moontide was shabby in spots—where it didn't show. They lived poorly—when they were alone, when Tony wasn't there to see. It was for him that Gloria put up a front." She became aware that the lieutenant had stopped talking and was looking at her. "I'm sorry. You were saying?"

"That Gloria was descended from black-skinned people and that Chandler wouldn't have been able to swallow that. He might believe that if they were married their child or children would be black. People still hold to that possibility, Doc?"

and he turned as he asked the question of Richard.

The doctor did not answer, seemed engrossed in another train of thought. He asked, "The other girl, the stepsister? She knew all this? Did her own snooping around, I imagine, and found out what Gloria was trying to hide. Well, since they were both fighting for the same man, why didn't she come out with it to Chandler?"

"We asked her that, in the short time that resident of yours gave us to talk to her. She couldn't tell Chandler. He thought she was a sweet, lovable character and she didn't want to spoil the 'image,' so she said. She was going to tell him. But she was waiting for just the right opportunity, was going to just seem to let it slip out, as though by accident.

"What she was getting a lot of enjoyment out of was holding it over Gloria's head. Gloria must have known she had to get rid of her. She waited until Julie came home from her date with Chandler, waylaid her and got her into the coach house on the pretext of having a talk about how she intended to give up Chandler, now that her great-grandmother had died, and even cried a little.

"Then, when she got Julie in there, the mask came off. She locked the door and kept Julie closed in and she had her innings. Taunted the other girl, told her she was going to die, another version of the cat-and-mouse game Julie had played with her. It went on for a long time. Gloria left the carriage house once, Miss Merrick told us, making sure her step-sister couldn't get out. She called to you, Miss Dexter. Said she wanted to get you down there. Kill two birds . . ."

He broke off. "Sorry. Wrong wording, wasn't it?"

"I'm beginning to think I can stand anything. Don't worry about it. I know now she tried to get me down there. But they were both overcome by the fumes, Gloria, too. Was it—was it a suicide attempt?"

"Hardly. She had Miss Merrick in the big old car and had turned on the exhaust. But the windows did not close properly. And when she tried to get out of the coach house, something had happened to the lock. It was old and rusty, and it stuck. She couldn't get out of the place. That's why we found her on the floor. The fumes felled not only her step-sister but they felled her, too. If we hadn't got there when we did . . ."

He was interrupted by Mrs. Dexter with a tray with cups of coffee on them. She looked agitated by the presence of a policeman in her living room but she made no excuses to linger there. She put the tray on a table and hastened out of the room.

The three sat drinking silently and after a while, when Rosalie had gathered up the empty cups and stacked them on top of each other, she said, "Gloria deliberately tried to make herself look like me and she took my coat when she went out to wait for Julie. So that I would have to wear hers. She wanted Azie and Jug to mistake her for me and vice versa, knowing that they would come after her once Mrs. Aldrich was dead. And she tried to kill me twice. Twice?" and her glance appealed for explanation.

"The first time was because she did not actually want a nurse here but knew it would seem suspicious if she refused to have one when her great-grandmother was dying. There were other nurses, weren't there?" the lieutenant asked. "Who didn't stay long? Perhaps she hoped the registry would give up sending any more. Any one of them might have noticed the scar on her patient's forehead and asked question about it of Mrs. Aldrich when she had periods of consciousness. And, knowing she was dying, she might have not have been reticent about telling what was behind the moon brand. I don't think you were meant to die that first time, merely to have been frightened off."

"And then," Rosalie put in, "I spoke about Hugo Bannister and mentioned how friendly he and I had been. And that was what marked me. I think Gloria may have gone back to his house after he died and made another attempt to get the manuscript and then figured I had it in my possession. It was missing because Benjamin, the manservant at the Bannister house, had sent it to me and it took a few days for it to be delivered.

"Part of it worked," she said, her voice becoming thinner, "because Azie was half blind and Jug was dim-witted. Gloria must have hoped that I would struggle and fight and that in order to make me submit, they would inflict physical violence on me, maybe even kill me in their zeal to brand their Malekala. Then they would be caught and sent away."

"No," the lieutenant said, "they would never have submitted to capture. They would have done away with themselves in a sort of hara kiri ritual. That, too, was a law of the Saluan tribe, according to Bannister's book. They would have had to commit suicide rather than submit to capture. Death rather than dishonor. Gloria knew that, too."

Rosalie had begun to shiver. "So she would have been rid of us all, if things had worked out for her. Julie, whose death would have looked like an accident. Me, supposed to have been killed by two savages, Jug and Azie by suicide. Then she would have married Tony and even if he found out the truth later and divorced her, she could have her alimony, in this case a form of blackmail."

She turned and looked at Richard. "I understand it all now. Except for one thing. Why did you ask for me especially to be put on that case? Gloria told me that you did."

"Then Gloria lied in one more respect. You mentioned this before. I did not, of course." He appeared a little angry. "I have no idea why she said that, unless she wanted to deflect your interest. It seems that Chandler was attracted to you, right from the start. Maybe she thought you weren't averse to a little flirtation, something to lighten the dull hours, and, if you believed I was interested in you, you'd turn your attention away from him and in another direction."

She was flushing again, furiously this time, and she hated the hot confusion of her senses. Looking away from Richard, she saw that the lieutenant was getting out of his chair. He said something about her signing the deposition, which she did. Then he picked up his hat and threw his topcoat over his arm.

She walked with him to the door and watched him get into the police car. It drove away, the sound of its motor and the unintelligible croaking of its radio growing fainter and fainter and finally dying away. Then, when she could delay no longer, she walked back into the living room.

Richard, who had arisen and was pacing back and forth, stopped when she got to the threshold and came toward her. He took her hand and pulled her into the room. They stook looking at each other while the mantle clock ticked into the silence and then, still wrapped in the spell of all she had heard, she said, "A long time ago a captain of a whaling ship kidnaped the daughter of a savage queen. How long ago? A hundred years or so? And that one act, that one crime, led to all this—murder and secrets and danger. It's like the echo of an old evil recurring in our lives."

Richard pulled her closer to him. "There are no more echoes," he said. "They're all gone now, darling. Listen!"

And she stood there and listened, but she did not hear anything. She looked up into his face and told him that.

"Music," he said. "Beautiful music. And bells ringing. And roman candles bursting. And if you tried hard enough, you could have smelled the flowers. And you could see the moonlight." He drew her over to the window and pointed out at the drab, cloud-shadowed day. "It isn't really like that out there," he said. "This is the prettiest day that ever was."

"Why, Richard!" she exclaimed. "I never would have believed it of you! Perhaps you're in the wrong business. Maybe you should be writing songs." She tried to make her voice light but it broke and all she could say was, "Oh, Richard. Oh, dearest!"

He led her back across the room where passersby could not catch a glimpse of a tall man taking a slender girl into his arms at this early morning hour. Now his mouth was the more ardent, his embrace clasped more strongly. It was his voice that murmured phrases of love against her lips.

Time stood still for a while and then they became conscious of it and he said, "They're waiting for me at the hospital," and she nodded because she understood.

He kissed her again, quickly and firmly, and then he left her to go to his patients. She knew that he would come back. She knew that he would always be going away into that other part of his life; and she knew, too, that he would always be coming back to the one they would share together.

The echoes of Moontide were completely gone, vanished into the dark, secret-filled past from which they had sprung.